ROADVIEW PUBLIC LIBRARY DISTR
2226 S. 16TH AVENUE
BROADVIEW, IL 60155-4000
(708) 345-1325

SEP 1 7 2001

Broadview Public Library District
2226 South 16th Ave.
Broadview, Illinois 60155
708-345-1325

GAYLORD M

Katrina

Katrina

Africa Fine

Five Star • Waterville, Maine

Copyright © 2001 by Africa Ragland Fine

All rights reserved.

This novel is a work of fiction. Names, characters, places, and incidents are either the product of the author's imagination, or, if real, used fictitiously.

Five Star First Edition Romance Series.

Published in 2001 in conjunction with Africa Fine.

Cover art by Will Walters.

Set in 11 pt. Plantin by Christina S. Huff.

Printed in the United States on permanent paper.

Library of Congress Cataloging-in-Publication Data

Fine, Africa 1972-
Katrina / Africa Fine.
p. cm. — (Five Star first edition romance series)
ISBN 0-7862-3027-4 (hc : alk. paper)
1. Racially mixed people—Fiction. 2. Afro-American men Fiction. 3. Milwaukee (Wis.)—Fiction. 4. Betrayal—Fiction. I. Title. II. Series.
PS3556.I4633 K38 2001
813′.6—dc21 00-050308

To Jeff, with Love

Many thanks to my friends and family, who have supported my dream. Special thanks to everyone who read version after version of this story, particularly the members of Florida Atlantic University's creative writing program.

And extra-special thanks to Johnny Payne—you helped me improve my writing tremendoulsy. You're not only a great writer, but a great teacher, too.

Chapter 1

The day Patrick came home was hot—the hottest day of the year. Katrina woke up late, feeling sticky and unrested, the fans set in two corners of the room doing nothing but blowing dust and making her sneeze. The old air conditioning unit emitted a low growl from the living room, a noise that would evolve into a roar by mid-afternoon. Hardly anyone had central air in Milwaukee—it just wasn't thought of most of the year. But every summer, August came as a surprise with its red sun that sprayed a glaze of moisture over everyone and everything. Sheets were always damp to the touch in August, and hair was always frizzed or flat.

Katrina willed her legs to move as she rolled out of bed, wiping soggy hair from her face. On days like this, when even lying naked directly underneath the air conditioner wouldn't be cool enough, she dreamed of cutting off all her hair. Trying to soothe her black curls into something acceptable was exhausting. If she shaved it off, she thought as she stood in the shower, letting the cool needles of water wash over her, her neck wouldn't sweat before she even got to work.

But she never did get up the nerve to cut it all off. Instead, she wore it tied back in a chignon every day until August became September and the yellow buses toted kids back to school.

She stepped out of the shower without drying and turned the fans so the air tickled her back while she surveyed the contents of her closet. She dreaded the feeling of pantyhose clinging to her legs like sausage casings, and the thought of wearing pants was equally unappealing. So she chose a long black skirt patterned with blue and white flowers and hoped her boss wouldn't notice her bare legs.

But Eléne probably *would* notice, since the obnoxious woman was aware of everything from sixty-one-minute lunch breaks to a misplaced comma in an informal interoffice email. Katrina had heard her boss referred to as "detail oriented," but "psychotically obsessive-compulsive" was the nicest way she could think to describe the woman.

At least it was Friday, so she'd have the next two days to forget about writing ads for companies she was lately either contemptuous of or overwhelmingly indifferent to. Two days without deciding whether to use an exclamation point or a period. Two days without arguing with her coworkers over the merits of past versus present tense. Two days of simulated freedom while she pretended she was a trust-fund baby who didn't have to do anything so petty as work for a living.

Katrina filled a mug with orange juice and shoved the morning paper into her briefcase before she ran out to her Mazda. As she opened the car door, she spilled the juice all over her shoes and bare legs and swore because she didn't have time to change. She shook the liquid off herself and slid into the car, where the compressed, still air assaulted her and the steering wheel burned her fingers.

She'd traded in her old Dodge Dart last winter, partly because she'd gotten her yearly raise and partly because her mother had convinced her that it was time to get a "real" car. Katrina had argued, noting that Annie was the one who'd bought her the Dart for her college graduation five years before, but now she was thankful for the Mazda sedan with its fully operational air conditioner. She turned it on full blast, weaving in and out of traffic to make it to work before anyone noticed she was late.

Once at her desk, Katrina wiped the last of the orange juice off her legs. She had just clicked on her computer to check her email when the phone buzzed.

"Katrina Larson," she answered.

"I thought you were going to call me back last night," her friend Chrissy complained, although her voice was cheerful.

Katrina leaned back in her chair and checked to make sure that her door was closed. "Good morning to you, too," she teased.

"I had some really good news to tell you."

"Sorry. My mom called and talked me to death. You know how she is, hassling me about dating. Mainly, the fact that I'm not."

Chrissy laughed. "Annie never changes. She's right, though. You never go out anymore."

"Anymore? I never went out. Not that much, anyway." She doodled on her note pad. "Don't you start in on me, too."

Chrissy ignored her. "I could fix you up with one of the other social workers here at the center. We could double."

Katrina shook her head and frowned into the phone. She would rather spend every Friday night alone than go on another date arranged by her mother or Chrissy.

"No thanks. The last blind date I had talked for an hour about his Rolex."

Chrissy snickered. "Don't blame that one on me. He was one of Annie's picks."

"Yeah, I'm still trying to recover. Anyway, I thought you said you had some big news." Katrina hated talking about her currently nonexistent love life.

"It's too much to explain over the phone," Chrissy gushed.

Katrina laughed. "Weren't you going to tell me last night on the phone?"

"Yeah, but you didn't call me back."

"Chrissy . . ." Katrina wasn't sure if Chrissy performed this circular logic on purpose to aggravate her, or if it somehow really made sense to her.

"Whatever—I can't wait to tell you all about it. Let's meet for lunch," Chrissy suggested. "My treat."

Katrina smiled at the excitement in Chrissy's voice. This must have to do with a new man. "Oh, Chris, I'm sorry, but I have a lunch meeting today. Why don't we hang out tomorrow?"

"What about tonight?"

All week, Katrina had been looking forward to Friday night and wearing as little clothing as possible while she watched a stupid movie on cable. She loved Chrissy, but she simply wasn't in the mood for company. Not tonight.

"I have some errands to run. Stuff I need to take care of." It was just a little lie, so Katrina felt only a little guilty. "But tomorrow, all day, I'm yours."

Chrissy sighed. "Okay, okay, tomorrow then."

"Good. I'll call you. And, by the way, what's his name?" Katrina teased.

Chrissy's voice was mockingly formal. "Rick Peres. But that's all you're getting—you'll have to hear the rest in person." Katrina laughed and hung up. She muddled through the rest of the workday in a haze of Diet Coke-fueled writing. She sneaked away from her desk at 4:49, hoping no one would come looking for her to solve some last-minute crisis that couldn't wait until Monday morning. In the parking lot, she tossed her briefcase into the trunk and turned the radio to an oldies station. She had mixed feelings about the fact that "Like a Virgin" was already considered an oldie, but she turned the volume up, matching Madonna on those little high notes in the chorus as she inched her way through traffic onto the highway.

It turned out it was an "all-Madonna Friday," and Katrina heard a significant sampling of the singer's catalog of hits as she sat in the motionless traffic, dreaming of the tall glass of ice water she'd have the minute she got home. She had belted out "Borderline," "Holiday" and "Into the Groove" and had performed particularly soulful renditions of "Live to Tell" and "Crazy for You" by the time she reached her exit. She pulled up in front of her apartment building and spotted her nosy neighbor Mrs. Collins bending over to peer at her potted plants.

"Hey, Mrs. Collins," Katrina called and waved before quickly closing the door behind her. Any more than that and she would have been trapped debating the use of pesticides with the woman for the next twenty-five minutes.

Inside, she peeled off her clothes, leaving them where they fell, and pulled on a pair of cut-off jeans and a tank top before pouring that glass of cold water.

It was late before she found a movie—*Pretty Woman.* It had just the right ingredients: beautiful hooker, handsome rich guy, happy-ever-after. It was a perfect fantasy world complete with opera and jewels. She grabbed a Popsicle and had just settled in to watch Julia Roberts work that long red dress when the doorbell rang.

She considered not answering it—it was 11:30, after all—but what if it was an emergency?

She sucked in her breath as she opened the door. It was Patrick. After five years. Patrick was back.

He wore frayed jeans, a blue and white striped shirt, short-sleeved, untucked, brand-new Nikes and an old Yankees baseball cap. He held a small black carry-on bag in one hand and a worn paperback book—Hemingway short stories—in the other. Katrina saw the tail lights of a taxi glowing down the street. He smelled tired, and she knew he'd come straight from the airport to her.

His dark and unruly Irish hair brushed the top of his collar and he'd grown a goatee that made him look younger than when she'd last seen him. His eyes were peaceful and he blinked slowly when he drew close. It was as if they hadn't been apart. His lips curved in the same smile, his cowlicks curled the same ways. Yet, his expression was more serious and a little guarded, the mark of experience, she guessed. They stood at her apartment door staring at each other, and Katrina wondered if she looked as splendid to him as he did to her.

He handed her the book. "For you." The cover was soft and worn, and when she looked inside, she saw *To Kim: "Hills Like White Elephants" is a great one. Love, Mom and Dad. 1975.*

She'd always liked used books, the idea that a book kept giving pleasure over the years as it changed hands, cities, maybe even countries. And she had always loved Hemingway, ever since she'd read *The Sun Also Rises* in the tenth grade. He'd remembered.

She thought about the last time she'd really spoken to Patrick at any length, during their final days in college. They had made plans to be roommates in a downtown apartment after graduation, to work all day and play all night. After spending four years at schools a thousand miles apart, they would be together again. They would find jobs, she in public relations or advertising, he at a newspaper or a magazine. And even though they hadn't ever discussed it, she'd hoped there would finally be more than friendship between them.

On the night before he was scheduled to come home, she was lying in her childhood room reading a book of Alice Walker short stories and wishing it were tomorrow already.

Patrick had called her from a Los Angeles Holiday Inn, where he'd driven with some college friends after his last day of classes at Stanford.

"We're going to bum around and travel this summer, before we get real jobs and settle down," he told her, the excitement making his voice catch. Hanging out in L.A. for a while was the first stop on their cross-country adventures, he said. "You understand, don't you?"

He never gave her a chance to answer, rambling on about how she should keep her eyes open for a newspaper gig for him for that fall. Before she could string together the words to hurt him the way he was hurting her, before she could figure out a way to say "I love you," he'd told her he missed her and hung up.

She didn't see him for five years. He sent her flowers on her birthday and they would talk briefly around major holidays. "Merry Christmas," he'd chime in her ear, his voice sounding full of vague cheer over the scratchy long-distance phone line. She would ask what he was doing, but all he ever told her was that he free-lanced for magazines she'd never heard of to support his traveling. She assumed he was still with one or two of those college friends she'd never met, but he avoided her questions, and she grew uncomfortable asking, something that had never happened before.

Friends forever, his occasional cards read. The irony made Katrina ache.

But she had proceeded as planned, forged ahead without him. She found an expensive apartment in a sketchy but up-and-coming downtown neighborhood. She took an underpaid sixty-hour-a-week advertising job with limited benefits and infinite potential. And each year she became more accustomed to the absence of Patrick.

Now here he was, standing on her front doorstep. She

wanted to slam the door and punish him for staying away. She wanted him to regret the five years they'd lost, wanted him to ask for forgiveness, wanted him to care that she felt abandoned. She wanted to hate him.

Instead, she molded her body to his and they kissed for the second time in their lives. He backed her against the open door, and after his hands came to rest on her hips. He tasted like oranges and they made love for the first time on her living room floor.

Later, the breeze coming through the open windows felt like menthol against Katrina's damp skin, so she led Patrick to the bedroom.

"I missed you," he said.

His words sounded like a voice inside her as she rested her head against his chest. Me, too, she thought.

"Where have you been?"

"Traveling. All over."

Their voices were husky and low, as if they were afraid of being overheard.

"What did you see?"

He talked about his travels, telling her about the sarong-clad men in Bali and eating ham and cheese baguettes in the cafés of Paris. He told stories of the trains in India stuffed with people and livestock, and he spoke to her in Korean. "God, I saw so many beautiful places. And each time, I thought of you."

Then why wasn't I with you, she thought. She thought about the things he hadn't mentioned, like whether he'd met anyone special in one of those beautiful places? She was afraid of the answer.

"Patrick."

"Mmm?" He was dozing.

"Why did you leave?"

A lengthy silence elapsed, and she wondered why he had to think so carefully about his answer. “I guess I needed to see the world a little. I mean, I figured I’d be coming back after the summer, but I kept traveling, and the next thing I knew five years had passed.”

She sighed. The five years hadn’t passed as quickly for her.

“Why did you come back?” The pause this time was infinite, and Katrina wondered if he was already asleep, or pretending to be. “I love you,” she whispered.

He moved closer and brushed his lips against her cheek. She hoped he couldn’t taste her tears.

“I love you, too.”

Katrina couldn’t sleep that night. She lay on her back, listening to Patrick snore lightly, thinking about him and that they had made love. Or had sex. She wasn’t sure what to call it. What would he call it? She wanted to wake him and ask him. But his sleeping face was too serene, too sweet.

She thought about seeing him again after all this time, the way she’d felt nervous and mad and excited and scared all at once. She remembered the way he had kissed her as they stood in her doorway, and she felt as if she was 12 again and experiencing their first kiss.

She’d tasted the Easter candy he’d been eating just before he bet her that she wouldn’t kiss him, bet her that she was scared. She had pretended to kiss him as a dare, but she really did it because she was charmed by the smudge of chocolate he’d gotten on the tip of his nose. That was when she decided they were meant to be, when she’d tasted the sweetness on his lips.

In the early days of their friendship, Patrick did more than take the place of the siblings Katrina never had, the classmates she never trusted, the cousins who never liked her. He made her feel she’d finally found a missing part of herself. They were the kind of friends who told each other everything, whose names are always mentioned as one: PatrickandKatrina. They were the kind of friends that she'd thought would stay that way forever. She cried over his poetry. She told him his stories stunk. He attended all her dance performances. He laughed at her love of math. She taught him to dance the merengue. He taught her to write love letters.

They were thirteen when Katrina got her first period. She raced straight from her bathroom and took the bus from the northwest side to the Flannerys' small wooden house near the river. The rooms always smelled of old records and the talcum Mrs. Flannery doused herself with, and ever since, the scent of baby powder had reminded Katrina of that day she'd dragged Patrick to a corner of the yard. She'd suddenly felt shy and picked paint off the wooden fence until Patrick cajoled her into telling. Her cheeks grew hot, and she was afraid to meet his eyes. Maybe he wouldn't want to play soccer anymore. Maybe this would ruin everything.

"Promise me this won't change things between us," she whispered, pinching his arm and remembering how other girls in her class had started to act differently once they had found blood on their panties.

Patrick hugged her and promised. "It doesn't mean anything," he assured her. Then he pushed her to the ground to get a sizable head start in a race to the playground nearby.

After that day, Patrick pointedly ignored her growing breasts and scoffed when other boys made comments. "It's just Katrina," he would tell them.

And now Patrick was lying next to her in bed, snoring, and everything had changed. She turned her back to him and just before dawn fell asleep. It was a light, troubled sleep that was destined to end prematurely and leave her unsatisfied.

They woke up early, and after Katrina left an apologetic message for Chrissy, headed to the lake before the sunburned matrons and mosquito-bitten children took over the beach. They staked out a place north of the rocks, picking a spot where the coarse sand was starting to dry after the morning dew.

The sun was already piercing, and they turned toward the city to try to stay cool, at least for a little while. They didn't talk much, as if they both wanted to ease into the day.

"Are you comfortable?" Patrick asked sweetly. "If you want water or something, just look in my backpack."

She smiled at him and nodded. After a while, Katrina dozed off. When she woke, the sun was high in the sky and her face was so hot it tingled. She turned onto her back, her elbows gritty with jagged sand, wishing for a cool breeze to brush away the heat. She gazed lazily out at the lake and watched kids jump in and out of the water. They floated like colorful buoys, kicking water at each other and screaming with laughter. With every splash, the musky scent of seaweed drifted through the air.

She turned her head slightly, watching Patrick gulp water from a long, ridged bottle. He held the cap loosely at his side, rolling it between his fingers each time he swallowed. The sun had darkened the freckles on his neck and back a bit more each year. Now, they were 27, and the spots stood out like tiny pennies against his golden skin.

The feel of August at the lake was familiar. As teenagers, they'd spent every summer Saturday at Lake Michigan, driving Patrick's rusted green Pinto, carrying two ratty old towels and a radio. Drowsy and languid, Katrina thought it was a shame that she'd avoided the lake while Patrick was away because it reminded her of him. Gazing at him as he put his water bottle aside, she buried his free hand in the sand, swept away the grains and started all over again.

Patrick turned to her and grinned. "What are you looking at?"

His voice was deep; she'd never really gotten used to how he sounded as an adult. When they'd first met on the playground at Holy Angels, he was the new kid who squeaked like a chipmunk. She squinted up at him without replying, sifting the sand absently.

"Well?" he demanded with mock impatience.

"Oh, so I can't look now?"

He laughed. "You can do anything you want to."

He picked up the water bottle and tipped it toward the sky, trying to catch those last drops on his tongue. His adult beauty was raw, and his sexuality seethed just below the surface, his every move casually confident. She'd known Patrick since he wore tight plaid shorts and a muddy pair of high-top Converse sneakers, and he was beautiful even then. He'd been a slight boy with curly blue-black hair, sly eyes the color of old quarters and a habit of nudging her when he thought something was funny and she didn't, as if an elbow to the ribs would set her on the path to good humor. By high school, he had become tall and rangy, but his lankiness was deceptive. During summers between college, Katrina had seen Patrick in bar fights after he'd had too much over-priced Heineken. Each time, his opponent had thought he had an easy battle only to be embarrassed, beaten, or, in one case, sent to the hospital. Katrina had refused to speak to him for a week after that fight, until he promised never to brawl again. She'd wanted him to promise not to drink, but Patrick Flannery said his ancestors would turn in their graves if he stopped drinking. She had rolled her eyes when he pulled out the old Irish stereotypes, and he just smiled because he knew how much she hated it.

Now, as Patrick eased down next to her on the blanket, his lips were close enough for his shallow breath to flutter her hair. Katrina squeezed a fistful of sand and thought his ancestors might be turning over in their graves anyway at the idea of Patrick with a ginger-skinned woman whose father was a former Black Panther and whose mother claimed to be half-Seminole, half a little bit of everything else.

He leaned over and kissed her softly. She kept her eyes open slightly even after he leaned back on the blanket, his hands under his head.

He glanced out at the lake. "Want to go for a swim?"

"Nope. I just want to lie here and enjoy the sun," she murmured.

Patrick smiled. "Remember all those summers we spent out here? I haven't been to the lake in years. Not since the summers during college."

She nodded. She didn't feel like telling him that she'd avoided the lake because of him. She just wanted to enjoy this moment.

He pecked her on the forehead before rising to his feet. "I'm glad we're back."

"Me, too."

He ran to the water, turning and waving to her before he paddled out deeper than Katrina liked. She watched him maneuver through the rolling waves, his arms slashing through the water as he swam parallel to the shore. She didn't swim, even though she'd taken countless lessons. In second grade, her friends had all been in the beginners' class, and if she had successfully demonstrated the back float, she would have been moved away from the few girls she was comfortable with. Now she could swim okay but only in a pool under supervision. So she watched while Patrick swam.

After a long while he reappeared on the shore, then at her side, soaked and smiling.

"Don't," she warned.

"Don't what?" he asked innocently, then shook his body, arms flailing, so water splashed all over her.

"You rat!" But she couldn't help laughing as she grabbed a towel.

"Just like old times, right? Wouldn't be a trip to the beach without getting a little wet," he said. When they were in high school, if he couldn't drag her into the shallow water, he did the next best thing, which was to drench her when he returned from a swim.

"Maybe there are *some* things about our past that we should just let go," she suggested.

"No chance." He plopped down next to her and propped himself up on an elbow.

"Now *you're* staring," she said.

He looked thoughtful.

"What?"

"I was thinking about last night," he said.

She smiled. "Don't start talking dirty. There are kids around."

He laughed. "I wasn't talking about the sex, silly. I was just thinking about something I never told you."

He looked serious, and she sat up. "What didn't you tell me?" She tried to stifle the alarm in her voice. He shook his head.

"It's nothing bad. It's good, really, I guess."

She lay back down, relieved, and turned on her side to face him. "So what is it?"

He began writing his name horizontally in the sand, using the "k" to draw her name vertically. He kept connecting their names in various permutations while she waited. He wasn't usually the one who was visibly uncomfortable. Usually, she was the one who worried and fidgeted, while he looked calm even when he wasn't.

"Last night, well, it wasn't completely an accident. Not that I came home for *that*. But I mean, I've thought about it before. Well, okay, that sounds weird. I just want you to know that I've had a crush on you forever. Since the first time we met."

She hoped her face didn't betray her surprise. She was pleased but wary. Was this revisionist history spun to fit their new relationship? But it didn't make sense for him to make up something like that. Not after they'd made love. He already had her. No lie was necessary. But she wasn't ready to spill her feelings, not yet. There were too many things that hadn't been said, like why he'd left her, why he'd stayed away so long, why he'd come back. They were questions that needed answers, but so far, he wasn't offering any.

Instead of speaking, he ran his fingers through her hair and kissed her on the cheek, the chin, the forehead and finally the lips, rubbing her shoulder gently while they kissed. They parted, laughing, when a toddler kicked sand in their hair, then giggled and ran away.

Chapter 2

Sunday morning Katrina slipped out of bed while Patrick still slept, pulling on her sweats, sneakers and a baseball cap for a run. She ran until her thighs tingled and her chest felt tight. She pushed herself beyond her normal thirty minutes, running for nearly twice that time, trying to loosen her shoulders and clear her head. While her feet slapped against the pavement, memories of her and Patrick kept pace in her mind.

They were sixteen when Patrick had sex for the first time. He drove his Pinto directly from his date's house to Katrina's. She greeted him on the back steps, shivering on a cool spring night in a green terry robe and her mom's threadbare slippers. Patrick covered her shoulders with his leather jacket and told her how he'd worried the girl would taste garlic on his breath from dinner. She'd asked lots of questions, her mouth open slightly in wonder at his answers. She almost wished she had done it first.

He finished telling the story and they sat quietly, avoiding each other's eyes.

"Promise me this won't change things between us," he mumbled.

"It doesn't mean anything," she sighed.

They never really talked about Patrick's sex life after that, and when other girls asked Katrina if she and Patrick were an item, she assured them that they were only friends. "It's just Patrick," she would say, rolling her eyes.

Their college acceptance letters both arrived on the same

day. They opened them together on the rocks by the lake. He would move a thousand miles away to Stanford, even though he couldn't afford to visit there before making his choice. Katrina had never been to California either, and she hadn't bothered to apply to Stanford after her guidance counselor told her she should set her sights lower. She would stay closer to home, go to the University of Illinois. They sat silently, and she wondered how life would go on without Patrickand-Katrina.

"Promise me this won't change things between us," they whispered. "It doesn't mean anything."

That was when she still believed that nothing would ever change between them, that growing older wouldn't threaten their closeness.

But now, growing older meant they could sleep with their limbs entwined, that he would say her name in a way he had never said it before, that she would taste the sweat on his skin.

His abrupt reentry into her life roused myriad emotions in her. Surprise. Confusion. Happiness. And, she realized, a little bit of anger that he hadn't given her any warning, hadn't allowed her to adjust slowly. He was just here, immediate and unavoidable. It didn't seem fair.

She walked the last half-mile back to her apartment, listening to her heart racing and ignoring the sweat dripping from her brow. Catching her breath, she walked into the bedroom and watched Patrick sleeping peacefully on the edge of the mattress. A tiny bit of spit dangled from the corner of his open mouth onto her new sheets, and at that moment Katrina hated him.

She kicked the side of the bed and was pleased to see him flail for mooring as his body teetered toward the floor. He barely managed to right himself and she felt a ping of disappointment.

"What?" He looked around, drowsy and red-eyed.

She stood there while his head cleared.

"Did you just kick the bed?" He eyed her uncertainly while she glared at him. "Katrina, what's wrong?"

He sat up and held his arms to her. She snarled and kicked the bed harder, just missing his right leg. Patrick jumped up, naked, and put on his boxers. They stood there, each waiting for the other to make the next move.

Katrina wiped the sweat off her face and pointed at him. "You can't come back here and pretend everything's okay. You can't come back and pretend you weren't gone for five years. Five fucking years!" She took a step forward with every sentence until she was standing close to him, her voice loud and angry.

"Katrina—"

She shook her head. "Whatever you're going to say, it's not good enough. I need to know why you left me and when you figured out you loved me. That's what I need to hear, and telling me how to say 'thank you' in Korean is not good enough." Suddenly realizing that she didn't want to share space with him, she backed away.

"Katrina."

"It's not good enough, Patrick." She stalked into the bathroom and turned on the shower. "I want you gone when I come out."

When Katrina twisted off the faucets, her palms were wrinkled and red and the water had turned cool. She felt calmer and wondered if her anger would cause Patrick to disappear for another five years.

She looked around the apartment for a note, but he'd left no trace that he had even been there. If her toe didn't throb from kicking the bed, she might have thought she'd imagined the whole thing. She put on a pair of jeans she hadn't worn in years and an old Stanford sweatshirt Patrick had sent her as a birthday present his sophomore year, and when she picked up the phone she realized that she still remembered the Flannerys' phone number: 555-4011. Before she could figure out what to say, Mrs. Flannery picked up.

"Hi, Mrs. Flannery. It's Katrina Larson."

She could hear shuffling in the background, a piece of paper being ripped and a hand covering the phone before Mrs. Flannery replied.

"Who?"

Katrina felt all her old antagonism toward Patrick's mother bubble up, and she marveled that the hostility was still mutual. Mrs. Flannery could be considered old, having waited until she was forty to have her only child, but she never forgot a name.

"Katrina Larson, Mrs. Flannery. Patrick's friend."

She heard Mrs. Flannery covering the phone and muttering. After about twenty seconds, Katrina wondered why she'd bothered calling. Mrs. Flannery had held a grudge against her ever since she and Patrick were in the seventh grade, when her mother called his mom a flat-footed bigot during parent–teacher night. Outraged at being identified as flat-footed in front of the entire room full of parents, teachers and kids, Mrs. Flannery had called Annie a half-breed. The two women had almost come to blows, stepping closer and closer to each other while yelling to be heard over the other's complaining. The three-hundred-pound football coach nearly tackled Annie to the ground trying to block the roundhouse punch she directed toward Ellen Flannery.

Since then, Mrs. Flannery had openly disapproved of Patrick's friendship with Katrina, pretending not to recognize her when she called and routinely ignoring her when she visited Patrick.

After more than a minute of unexplained muffling of the receiver, Mrs. Flannery came back on the line. "Hello?" Her voice was pleasant and expectant, as if she'd just answered the phone and expected the caller to be one of those nice Catholic girls from Holy Angels parish.

Katrina sighed. "Hello, Mrs. Flannery. Is Patrick there? Can I speak to him?"

Patrick's mother dropped the phone, and he picked up immediately.

"Hey."

"Hey." Katrina didn't know what to say. "It's good to see your mother hasn't changed."

"Yeah, it's like a time warp over here. I think I see my eighth grade report card on the refrigerator."

She wanted to laugh but couldn't. "Are you busy?"

"Just dodging my mother's scissors. She insists my hair is too long. Says I look like a hippie."

"Do they still have hippies?"

"In my mother's world they do."

She took a deep breath. "Can we talk?"

"You weren't interested in talking this morning."

"I know. I'm sorry. Would you come over?"

"Only if you promise not to kick me."

This time she did laugh. "Promise. See you in a while."

By the time Patrick arrived, Katrina had brewed and dumped out two full pots of coffee in an effort to stop her hands from shaking. Even though she'd used up all her coffee beans, she offered Patrick a cup and was relieved when he said no thank you.

They sat on opposite ends of her brown leather sofa, avoiding each other's eyes.

"Patrick, I need to explain what happened this morning." She thought she had been unfair. She wanted to know more about his life, but she felt bad for lying in his arms, then kicking him for it.

"I think that's obvious. You didn't want me here." He looked uneasy.

She shook her head. "That's not true. I wanted you too much." There. She'd said it. She hated herself for wanting him so badly, for not demanding more answers in exchange for the softness of his hands on her skin. She watched his fingers trace the stitches on the leg of his jeans.

"I just have a lot of things to sort out. A lot of things to get straight in my head. I know it's not fair to you, but it's the truth."

She needed a better explanation than that. "That's such a cliché, Patrick."

He bowed his head and rested his forehead in his palms.

"I know. But I need some time."

He looked up, his eyes the color of faded denim, full of pleading and a touch of melancholy.

All she could think was that she'd do anything for him. He moved closer, and she remembered the way his lips felt against the small of her back.

"I don't want to think about the past or the future yet. I need to figure out where I am right now. Is that okay?"

The past and the future were the only things Katrina wanted to talk about. The present felt too heavy. "I don't know if it's okay." She studied the chipped polish on her toenails.

"I'm here now. What difference does all that other stuff make when I love you as much as I do?" He reached over, brushed her hair off her forehead with his fingertips, and Katrina did her best to forget why "all that other stuff" mattered.

PatrickandKatrina spent the rest of the weekend getting to

know each other's bodies the way they'd once known each other's thoughts. As she fell asleep curled against his back that Sunday night, she decided to ignore her doubts and simply be happy.

Katrina found herself listening to the sidewalk outside her door for signs of him when he wasn't with her. It was only a week since he'd been back. Seven days and she'd seen him on each one. Still, it wasn't enough. She wanted to cover herself with Patrick, immerse herself in him until it made up for all the time they'd spent apart.

But she didn't want to seem overeager, so she didn't call him on the eighth morning. It was a Saturday, and she decided to spend the day shopping. Or reading. Or playing tennis. Something.

Katrina's air conditioning was on full blast, so she couldn't feel the heat wavering outside her apartment. But as she walked from room to room getting dressed, ironing, toasting a bagel, she caught glimpses of her neighbors outside. She lived in a cluster of 2-story buildings that held four apartments each. Patches of manicured lawn separated the cream-colored brick buildings, and she lived on the first floor. She stopped at the small side window in the kitchen, wondering how hot it was but not wanting to step outside just yet.

She watched as Mrs. Collins watered the potted tulips on her tiny patio, a fine sheen of sweat glossing her wide, flat face. Her yellow golf shirt clung to her broad shoulders and dark, wet patches dotted the creases of her snug Bermuda shorts. She looked up from her watering can to greet Sam Walsh, who ran the corner grocery store. He insisted that Katrina call him Sam even though he was at least seventy-five and Katrina's mother had taught her to address her elders respectfully. Sam wore jeans, which was a relief since he was exposing more than enough flesh in his thin Hanes tank top. Mrs. Collins and Sam spoke cordially for a moment, she sprinkling the sidewalk with water as she gestured with the watering can. He lifted the hem of his shirt to wipe his brow, leaving a smudge and alarming Katrina with the sight of his concave, wrinkled stomach.

So it was hot, and she went to trade her dark blue T-shirt for a lighter halter. She decided to go shopping and was on her way out the door when the phone rang. It was Patrick, and she felt a jolt of happiness at hearing his voice. She perched on the end of her sofa and cradled the phone on her shoulder, but before she could begin the pleasantries to start the conversation, he drowned her out.

"Hey, want to go on a date?"

She smiled to herself. It sounded so high school and yet satisfying. Their first date. "Sure. Where are we going?"

"I thought maybe a drive down to the lake, dinner, and then the boys were talking about having a little party for me later," he said. He was breathless and cheerful, and she suspected that he felt like making up for lost time, too. But what boys could he have rounded up in a week?

"The boys?"

"You remember Carl, Mike and Joe from high school? I called them up to see if they were still around, and they want to have a little reunion."

She hesitated. When Katrina and Patrick had graduated from eighth grade at Holy Angels, they'd both gone on to attend Regis Catholic High School. Around that same time, when Patrick first saw a shadow over his lip, he decided he needed to hang around with more guys and less Katrina. She let him go without much protest, knowing he'd be back.

He'd latched on to a group of jocks that included Carl

Reyes, Mike Lomax and Joe Johnson. Carl was an overweight, acne-stricken kid who towered over every other ninth grader, and he was defensive about it. By sheer size he made the varsity football team, where he was a third-string linebacker, and he relished the opportunity to physically abuse smaller kids. Even though Patrick hadn't hit his growth spurt and was still skinny, Carl protected him like a little brother.

Mike had also played football, but he was tall and thin and prided himself on what he called his "smooth moves." Eventually he became the star quarterback on the Rams' losing team, but when he was a freshman he never even got in a JV game. To make up for it, Mike slicked his hair back with gel until it formed a helmet with a little duck tail in back. He cultivated a smile he thought was charming and he winked and pointed at the girls as they passed him in the halls.

Joe was Katrina's favorite of the three, although she was vaguely suspicious of the fact that he had started calling himself José during the two months when it was cool to be Puerto Rican at Regis. After that, he was just Joe again. He played tennis, and people said he would be a pro someday. But he never talked about it because he never said much, just shrugged and smiled shyly, rubbing his curly hair, when asked a personal question. When he did say something, he was quiet and polite, and Katrina could never figure out why he hung out with Mike and Carl.

In high school those two had regarded Katrina suspiciously, becoming silent and shifty when she tried to talk to Patrick while they were around. So Katrina had backed off, letting Patrick have his "boys" while she pretended to like a group of girls who wore too much makeup and dreamed of being varsity cheerleaders. Cheerleading was never at the top of Katrina's list of things to covet—she had never been considered perky—but she pretended to think electric blue eyeliner was a good idea and she secretly applauded the fact that no girl could be on the varsity cheerleading squad until junior year.

Eventually Patrick out-grew Mike and Carl, although throughout the rest of high school and college he'd remained friendly with Joe, seeing Carl and Mike when he needed a shot of goofy testosterone. He and Katrina had resumed the closeness briefly interrupted by his semester-long flirtation with male bonding.

Now, Joe, Mike and Carl were welcoming Patrick. She'd seen them around once in a while, at the grocery store or at the mall, but they seldom talked beyond a quick hello.

Still, she didn't want to spoil Patrick's first days back in town.

"Sounds great! I'm on my way out now, but let's have dinner later," she said.

"Perfect."

There was an awkward moment while they each waited for the other to wrap things up. Then they both laughed a little, and he cleared his throat.

"Hey, have I told you how much I missed you while I was gone?"

She could hear his smile. "About a million times. But I'm up for a million and one."

"I missed you." He was quiet and serious.

"I still feel like we need to make up for lost time, you know?"

"That's why you should let me come take you out for ice cream. I don't want to wait until dinnertime to see you," he said lightly.

"Ice cream? It's not even noon yet."

"So? It's hot out there. And mint chocolate chip is good at any time of the day. Please?"

She laughed. "Oh, all right. But you're buying."

"I wouldn't have it any other way. See you in twenty minutes."

That night they gorged themselves on eggplant parmesan and hot garlic rolls, and Patrick insisted on paying. They'd sat at a small corner table, so close their knees brushed. He spent the evening looking at her as if he wanted to etch her face into his memory, quietly quizzing her about her life, asking the tiniest details: How often did she work out? Was mauve still her favorite color? Was her mother still trying to run her life? He held her hand in the parking lot on the way to her car. Even though she believed that women shouldn't wait for men to pay their way, she liked the attention. She liked it when he rushed to open the driver's side door for her and helped her in. Katrina smiled to herself as she leaned over to unlock the passenger door and thought that in the movies, the man would be driving. But in this real-life fairy tale, Prince Charming had been out of the country for five years and didn't own a car.

She started the car, and by silent, mutual consent, they opened all the windows to let warm, thick air swirl around them, even though the night was moist and nearly as hot as it had been that morning. She started the car and turned to Patrick. "This was a great date."

He nodded and took her hand, as if he couldn't bear not to be touching her at all times. "It's been fantastic." He softly rubbed her palm with his thumb, tilting his head to look at her. "And I can't wait until later, after the party."

She wanted to say that they shouldn't wait until later. She wanted to tell him to call Carl and make up some excuse. She was about to suggest that they had too much time to make up for to waste precious hours at a party with old high school buddies.

Reading her face, he smiled and shook his head. "I know what you're thinking, and believe me, I'd rather take you straight home. But the guys have got this whole thing planned, and I'd feel like a jerk canceling at the last minute."

She leaned over and kissed him. She felt him resisting, but as soon as he relaxed into her, she pulled away. "You're sure you don't want to go straight home?" she whispered.

He groaned. "You are so evil."

"Evil enough to convince you?"

He pointed at the steering wheel. "Come on, you know I can't. We'll only stay for a while, I promise."

She shrugged and smiled. "It was worth a try. To Carl's house we go. But you'd better make it up to me later."

"You know I will."

Sitting in Carl's cramped living room, Katrina looked around at the late-seventies-era brown carpet and felt as if she'd been transported back to high school. She'd hoped Patrick's buddies would surprise her by being completely changed. During the drive over, she imagined Carl as thin, neat and responsible, maybe an insurance agent or an accountant. Mike, she imagined, could own a restaurant or sporting goods store and be very polite. She hoped Joe had come out of his shell, maybe even acknowledging his Latino heritage by reverting to José.

Their adherence to personality structures formed years ago disappointed her. Carl was even fatter and had lost any slight athleticism he'd once had. Mike's flirtatious arrogance seemed pathetic all these years later. Joe was Joe, quiet and smiling, and he was the only one who seemed remotely happy, although Katrina couldn't tell for sure since he still shied from prolonged conversation.

Just like old times, Carl, Mike and Joe said the briefest

hellos possible to Katrina before settling into the familiar patterns of male interaction. She noted their girlfriends seemed to feel the same lack of interest in Katrina that she had for them. She tried to be nice to these other token women who were also being ignored by their respective boyfriends, a fact that vindicated Katrina. They were indifferent to any woman, not just her.

"Hey," Katrina nodded at the other girlfriends, trying not to stare at the way their permed hair had stiffened into wings around their faces.

"Hi," they mumbled back. The women stood there silently listening to the guys punch each other's arms and laugh. Finally, Katrina turned to one of the girlfriends.

"So, did you go to Regis?"

The woman took a swig from her bottle of Zima. "Nope. Saint Bonaventure. Want a Zima?" She held the bottle out invitingly.

"No thanks. Maybe later." Right. Maybe later when she was living in the Gobi Desert and Zima was the only liquid standing between her and certain death.

A woman wearing a pink golf shirt and matching jeans offered helpfully, "We've got a whole case in the cooler out back." Katrina forced a smile that she hoped was appreciative.

"Great. Thanks."

In between tepid conversation with the other women, she watched the guys and thought that only Patrick had changed from the boy he had been. During breaks in Mike's monologue about his plans to eventually go into business for himself, Patrick came over to rub Katrina's shoulders or bring her a basket of pretzels. He managed to simultaneously sound interested in Carl's recap of old high school football plays while smiling over at Katrina, mouthing "I love you." They all listened to Joe's brief discussion of his job as a math teacher at their old high school.

Patrick managed to make everyone feel special without slighting anyone. He'd always been charismatic and likable, but she had never seen him take over a room the way he did tonight. Even the girlfriends giggled and preened at his teasing compliments.

True to his word, in under two hours Patrick caught up on his old friends' lives, sipped a couple of beers and told an anecdote about a misunderstanding in Amsterdam that stranded him in an unfamiliar section of the city with no money and no transportation for six hours. They left the party with Patrick promising to get together soon with his buddies.

As they pulled away from the curb, he rolled down his window and breathed deeply. "No matter where I went, no place ever smelled quite like home, you know?" He turned to Katrina. "That wasn't so bad, was it?"

She considered it. "Well, those girls were boring, Mike, Carl and Joe are the same as ever and I don't really like Zima or pretzels." They came to a light, and she glanced over at him and smiled. "Nope, it wasn't that bad."

"Thanks for hanging in there. I couldn't disappoint the guys, and it was kind of nice to see them. Weird, but nice."

"Weird as in they haven't changed much since high school?" she ventured.

"Weird as in I guess I *have* changed a lot since high school," he nodded. "So many things that used to interest me just don't anymore."

Her back tensed, and they rode silently the rest of the drive back to her apartment. As she put the car in park and turned off the ignition, she looked at him. "I hope not everything about you has changed. I mean, I hope *some* things from your past have held your interest," she said.

He took her hand and brought it softly to his lips. "The things I love, the people I love—that will never change."

"Never?"

"Never."

Chapter 3

During the next few weeks, being happy meant going to the beach with Patrick, burying his hands in the sand. It meant rushing home from work every day, looking forward to touching his fingertips as they watched a movie. It meant getting to know Patrick and letting him know her after so much time apart.

"Hey, have you started looking for a job yet?" Katrina asked one night as they munched tacos and watched baseball on her living room floor. She hoped it didn't sound like "Are you staying?" even though that's what she really wanted to know.

Patrick picked the onions out of his Taco Supreme and considered the question. "Well, Mom needs someone around the house now that Dad's slowing down, and I'm not quite sure what I want to do yet, so I think I'm just going to hang out right now." He took an enormous bite of his onion-free taco and smiled at her. "More time for us to be together," he mumbled through a mouthful of processed meat and shredded lettuce.

"You've got a piece of tortilla stuck to your cheek," Katrina informed him, laughing. "I wish I had my camera, you slob."

He removed the tortilla, pretended he was going to shove it in his mouth with the rest, then flicked it at her at the last minute.

"Now *you've* got a piece of tortilla stuck in your hair," he said with mock seriousness.

Katrina shook her head and sipped her Pepsi. "It's almost like you're still 12 years old, Patrick," she said, rolling her eyes. She daintily set her drink down on the carpet, cut a slice of Mexican pizza and tossed it at him.

"Arrrrgh!"

She snickered as he scraped bits of refried bean off his goatee.

"See, these are the good times we would miss if I had a job," he said.

"Right. Now shut up and eat—the Brewers are up."

When they were kids, Katrina and Patrick had always watched baseball games together. He was a Yankees fan, but they liked to spend summer days at County Stadium watching Paul Molitor field grounders for the Brewers. It was one of their childhood traditions until college, when watching baseball suddenly seemed like a waste of precious warm days.

Katrina spent four years of college wishing she had been smart enough and brave enough to go to Stanford. She made some friends, and she actually liked her roommate Chrissy, despite her long blond hair, perfectly petite body and penchant for asking Katrina about the habits and customs of black people. Chrissy was from northern Wisconsin, where the only dark-skinned people were the broad-shouldered men who played for the Green Bay Packers, and even they didn't hang around much after football season. But Chrissy was sweet and shared Katrina's love for peanut butter cookies, so they became friends.

During her first year, Katrina wrote occasionally truthful letters to her mother and Patrick about her life. She assured Patrick that she was managing fine without him.

"I've never had so much fun in my life," she gushed in her

weekly missives. Curled up on the squeaky twin bed munching on Triscuits, she concocted tales of daring and debauchery while post-adolescent parties raged outside her dorm room. While she sat writing, girls froze wearing mini-skirts and tank tops on icy November nights, and boys spent their fathers' money on cheap gin and cigarettes they couldn't inhale. Sitting in her overheated room, she missed Patrick desperately.

Chrissy caught her crying one night and sat down on Katrina's bed. "What's wrong, Kat?"

She was too upset to tell Chrissy that she hated to be called Kat. "Nothing."

"You're sitting here on a Saturday night alone, crying. Something must be wrong."

She had told Chrissy the bare necessities about Patrick, that he was her best friend and they'd grown up together in Milwaukee. She didn't say anything about love or the future, but Chrissy wasn't dumb.

"It's Patrick, huh? You miss him."

She shrugged, looking away.

"Hon, I know it's hard to be away from your boyfriend, especially when he's so far away, but you have to try and enjoy yourself while you're here," Chrissy said.

Katrina felt pathetic. She sat up, wiping her cheeks. "He's not my boyfriend."

Chrissy looked at her doubtfully. "Kat, I know you don't like to get too personal, but you can talk to me."

"There's nothing to talk about. Patrick's my friend and I miss him. That's all."

Chrissy didn't push. She seemed to understand Katrina's denial. "Well, it's okay to miss your friends, but what I said still stands—college only happens once." Chrissy rubbed her shoulders. "Now, let's get out of this stuffy room and go get something to eat, okay?"

She knew Chrissy was right. Patrick wasn't sitting around crying over her. His letters were full of fun. He raved about writing articles for the Stanford student newspaper. He gave play-by-play analyses of his intramural basketball games. He went on for pages about his literature classes and the virtues of Chaucer. She examined his letters carefully, looking for evidence that he was as lonely as she, but all she found was his happiness. She was sure he missed her; she never doubted his friendship. But his life wasn't standing still.

Chrissy wasn't the only one worried about Katrina. Patrick may have been fooled by the enthusiastic letters, but her mother wasn't.

"Katrina, why don't you come home for the weekend? It's not even an hour away."

She limited her trips home to Milwaukee because she wasn't sure she could face Annie's mothering more than one weekend a month.

"Mom, I'm all right. You worry too much."

"You're my baby. I can't help but worry about you, down there all alone."

"There are, like, thirty thousand students here."

Annie would not be distracted. "You know what I mean, Katrina. You don't talk much about your friends or parties and dating."

"Mom, I call and write you all the time, and we've talked about Chrissy and some of the other girls in my dorm. And anyway, who talks to their mother about parties and guys?" She wished she were a better liar. She could feel her mother preparing one of her lectures in the static-filled silence.

"Okay, let's be honest. Your letters are bullshit."

"Mom!" She was uneasy. When Annie cursed, she meant business. When Katrina was a little girl, her father had once told her that Annie used to curse like an angry Marine, but the Annie Katrina had grown up with only used profanity when there was about to be trouble.

"You're my only child, and for years it's been just you and me. I know when things aren't right with you."

Katrina took a deep breath. "I guess it's all a little overwhelming. My first time away from home, away from you."

"Away from Patrick," Annie added.

Katrina paused. No way was she was going to talk to her mother about Patrick. Some things were not meant to be shared.

"Of course I miss Patrick. I miss all my friends from high school." Katrina's voice quavered. It happened every time she tried to fool Annie. "And even if I did want to come home this weekend, I wouldn't have a ride."

"So I'll come get you, of course. You know all you have to do is ask." Annie's voice was efficient and comforting. She had a way of putting Katrina's problems into perspective, making the melodrama seem manageable.

"It'll be good to see you, Mom."

"You too, honey."

Katrina hung up and pulled out her box of stationery to write Patrick another letter.

That first college summer was a relief. When school was out, she didn't have to pretend she was having fun, pretend she didn't miss Patrick. She felt like her old self again.

Katrina had exchanged addresses with Chrissy and they promised to keep in touch. Patrick had an internship at a semi-reputable neighborhood newspaper, and she worked as an editorial assistant at an ad agency. Each Friday night they sat on the swing in her backyard, trying to top each other's office horror stories. Most Saturday nights they saw big-budget action thrillers or sappy romantic comedies at the dollar theater. They spent the last night of the summer at the lake, dipping their toes into water that was already cooling off for the fall.

"I don't know what I would have done without your letters," Patrick said, making the water swirl with his big toe.

"What do you mean?"

"I was lonely, being so far away from home and everything. It was hard, but knowing that you were having so much fun made it better."

She felt bad for deceiving him, but she couldn't think of a way to tell him the truth. "But you wrote about all the great things you were doing. Wasn't it true?"

"Yeah, I did all that stuff—basketball and writing for the paper—but it's not the same when you're not there to share it with me." He looked up at her with a sad smile.

Now she could never tell him that most of her letters were fiction—his were all true. She nodded. "I missed you lots, too."

She pulled her feet from the water, rubbing her toes to warm them.

"Sometimes I wish I hadn't gone so far away to school," he said.

She thought about all the nights she'd spent wondering what he was doing, and with whom. "Sometimes I wish I had gone with you."

He grasped her hand and measured her fingers against his.

"Do you think it's changing things between us?" he asked quietly.

She looked at the water bubbling darkly over the rocks. The occasional splash of a fish broke its rhythms, but the lake never changed. It grew older, but it still tasted metallic, still ran cool even on the hottest days.

"No. It doesn't mean anything," she said weakly.

Later, they hugged and promised to do the same thing next summer, and it wasn't so hard to say good-bye.

She remembered that summer clearly one weekday afternoon as she sat trapped inside her cramped, airless office pretending to care about advertising dollars, image and market share. Katrina's mind filled with uneasy thoughts—doubts about her life, about Patrick. She wondered whether he was avoiding work because he truly wanted to help his parents or if there was more to it. Doodling on her lined yellow pad and ignoring the bleep of incoming emails, she considered whether it was because he wasn't back for good, that she was just a pit-stop.

Maybe he had something waiting for him overseas. Or someone. But he would have told her, wouldn't he? When they were kids, he'd always been so sunny and open, always saying that she was the only person who knew all his secrets. Now he was still often sunny, but there were things he wasn't saying. She wondered how important those things were.

She glanced at the clock. It was 2:33, and she wished she could slip out unnoticed and leave for the day. She called Patrick, half hoping he wasn't home. She worried that if they talked while she was in this mood she might demand answers to the questions that nibbled at the edges of their reunion. But she couldn't resist—she needed to hear his voice. She listened impatiently while the phone rang again and again, wishing Mr. Flannery would occasionally answer the phone, praying that she wouldn't have to deal with Patrick's mother.

"Hello?"

"Patrick."

"Hey. How's the working world?"

"Boring, as usual. How many cigarette ads can one person write?" She rubbed her temples. "I don't even smoke."

"Remember how pissed you got at me when I started smoking my dad's cigarettes in high school?"

"You stank like some old bum! I refused to talk to you until you stopped." She smiled at the memory of Patrick trying to conceal the cigarette burns on his jeans by ripping the holes wider and pretended he'd meant to do that all along.

"You know, maybe you should seriously think about doing something else." She'd told him how she dreaded going in to work every day. Suggested a different kind of writing, maybe journalism, or public relations for a non-profit. But change was hard for Katrina.

She sighed. "I know, I know, but this job pays so much money and I've been here for almost five years. Forget it. Let's talk about something else. I'm tired of whining," she said. "What are you up to?"

"Thinking about you," he said suggestively.

Katrina laughed. "All day?"

"Every day."

"Well, in between thinking about what a babe I am, what else are you doing?"

"My mother is introducing me to the wonderful world of lawn maintenance," he drawled. "It's the sport of the future, you know."

"Hmm. Sounds incredibly interesting." She decided to test the waters, feel him out a bit. "Maybe you should consider getting out of there and finding a job that'll keep you busy during prime lawn maintenance time," she ventured.

He hesitated, then said, "Why do you keep pushing me about that?"

She was startled. "I didn't mean anything by it. Most people have jobs, so I figured you might get one, too. You don't have to get upset."

She heard the smile in his voice. "Sorry. I'm not upset. I just haven't figured all that out yet, so I can't really give you a good answer. You may be right, though. I just don't know if I'm ready yet."

She felt her throat tighten. "Ready?"

"For the commitment."

Was he talking about her? She took a deep breath to stay calm.

"Well, you only got back a few weeks ago. It must be hard to adjust after being away for so long."

She could almost hear his mind working, reading into her words. He took his time answering. "It's a little weird. Especially with us, you know? This all took me by surprise."

She frowned. He sounded as if he was the only one taken by surprise, like he was trying to justify something to her, to himself.

She snapped at him without meaning to. "It's weird for both of us. I didn't expect this, either."

He sighed. "I know. I didn't mean anything by that."

There weren't these uncomfortable silences between them in the past, the words that came out wrong and put the other person on guard. Sex added to their relationship, but it also took some things away.

She tapped her pen on the desk and wondered what all this had to do with getting a job, anyway. What did all this have to do with PatrickandKatrina? She rubbed her forehead to clear her thoughts.

"I don't know how we got here, but I don't want to argue with you. I want things to be good between us," she said, trying to make peace.

"I love you. You know that. And as far as a job goes, it probably would be easier for me to work a twelve-hour day, but my parents, especially Mom, they need me."

Katrina figured Mrs. Flannery wasn't that needy, but she didn't want to get into a heavy discussion about Patrick's overbearing mother.

"I guess your dad's ecstatic to have you as a buffer from your mom, huh?"

"If he ever spoke, I'm sure he'd express pleasure and gratitude."

"He's still the quiet type, I gather."

"After being married to my mother for forty years, who wouldn't be?"

She could hear Mrs. Flannery yelling in the background. "That's her now, it sounds like."

"Yeah, I think I've spent my allotted ten minutes on the phone, and she wants me to get back to weeding," Patrick laughed. "I'd better go before her gallbladder bursts or something."

Katrina grinned. "Forget writing cigarette ads—I think it's bad karma to wish gallbladder problems on your mother."

"Wish? I never said wish. So, will I see you tonight?"

"I'd love to, but I've got a date with my mother," Katrina said. "I haven't seen her in a month, and she's not happy."

"She does live all the way up in Madison. Tell her you've been working overtime or something."

"Madison's only an hour and a half away from here, and she's not going to buy it. No, I'm in for a night of guilt. And I told her about the return of the prodigal son, so I'm sure she's full of probing questions about you that are none of her business."

"I'll take my gallbladder-popping mother any day over a nosy, pissed-off Annie Larson. Have fun," Patrick said, calling good-bye over his mother's cackling orders.

Katrina shook her head, smiling. She looked at the clock and got back to work.

Chapter 4

"My goodness, I think you're taller than the last time I saw you!" Annie exclaimed as she opened the screen door and enveloped her daughter in a bear hug.

Katrina pecked her mother on the cheek. "Mom, it hasn't been *that* long since I visited. And, I'm twenty-seven, which means I've probably finished growing."

"Oh, it must be about six months now since I saw you last. Want some lemonade?"

"Try six weeks, if that. And yes, I'll have some lemonade."

Katrina sat on her mother's old but immaculate flowered sofa and looked around. It continually amazed her that even though her mother had moved from Milwaukee to the suburbs of Madison just a few years ago, she'd managed to make this small house look just like Katrina's childhood home.

It was like stepping back into time. Annie had managed to find oak floors the exact shade of those in their old house, had hung Katrina's prom picture and high school graduation cap on the wall next to her college diploma with the same precision and somehow found the identical shade of yellow for her kitchen and dining room.

Seeing the kitchen reminded Katrina of the time her mother had first decided that yellow was the appropriate color to accompany food preparation. She was nine years old, lying awake in the tiny pink bedroom she'd decorated herself. She had been startled from sleep by the sound of breaking glass. Groggy, she recognized the sound of her drunken father fumbling in the kitchen. He always thought he could sneak in and fix himself something to eat without Annie noticing. He invariably broke one of her special dishes or expensive glasses, waking up the house.

She flinched at the sound of her parents' loud voices. She covered her head with a pillow and waited for it to be over.

"Goddammit, Earl! You can't come in and out of here when you feel like it!" Annie spat.

"Ann, come on. I was just out with the boys. What's the big deal?" Earl's voice was slurred and sweet.

Katrina felt a familiar knot in her stomach and pulled herself into a ball. She knew this argument almost by heart.

"The big deal, Earl, is that you have a child. And a home. And a wife. You owe us more respect than this."

Katrina heard her father's uncertain footsteps on the linoleum floor.

"Baby, I'm sorry, okay? It's just been a long week. I needed to blow off some steam."

"I worry about you when you're out so late." Annie sounded calmer.

"I know. I promise to call next time," Katrina's father said.

She could hear the sound of kissing and wondered who was kissing whom.

"Earl, get off me."

"Don't be mad, Ann."

"I'm not mad. I'm disappointed."

Katrina heard her father pull a chair away from the table, making a screeching sound, sure to leave a black mark.

"Earl, be careful of the floor!"

He sighed. "Jesus Christ, it's always something. I just need to sit down. I had a little too much to drink."

"No kidding."

Katrina heard the swish of the broom and the tinkle of tiny pieces of glass.

After a few minutes, Annie said, "Earl, just come to bed. I don't want Katrina to find you passed out at the kitchen table when she wakes up."

Katrina rolled over and tried to sleep.

The next morning, her mother had laughed at her father's corny jokes. Her father had winked at her conspiratorially, as if to reassure her. She ate her cornflakes in silence, looking around the kitchen at the spotless white walls for evidence of last night's fight.

Earl finished his breakfast and kissed Annie on the cheek. "Ladies, the grass is looking a little shaggy, so I'm going out to do some yard work," he announced. Passing by Katrina's chair, he paused to kiss her on the forehead and whisper in her ear. "I love you. Everything's going to be all right."

Her mother had taken her shopping that morning after breakfast.

In the car on the way to Marshall Fields, Annie glanced over at Katrina. "You sure are quiet today."

She shrugged, looking out the window at the other cars whizzing by on the highway.

Annie frowned. "How did you sleep last night?"

"Okay, I guess."

"Did you hear your father come in?"

Katrina shrugged again.

"Adults have fights sometimes. It's just how it is."

She looked at her mother. "You and Daddy have a lot of fights."

"That's true, I suppose. But we love each other. You know that."

"Then how come you can't get along?"

Annie pursed her lips. "Well, loving someone doesn't

mean you always agree. You never met my mother, your grandmother—she passed away before you were born. But she and I, we never got along, even when I was as small as you."

Katrina thought for a moment as they turned into the mall parking lot. "How come you didn't get along with your mom?"

"Oh, it's a long story. She didn't approve of anything I did. I think my marrying your father was the last straw." Annie pulled smoothly into a parking space. "But the point is, I still loved her. And she still loved me. Just like me and your dad."

Annie turned off the car and reached over with both hands to stroke Katrina's cheeks. "Do you understand?"

She never forgot the look in her mother's eyes. It was as if she wanted something so badly, something she knew she would never have.

"Mom? Is Dad going to leave us?"

A tear floated down to Annie's chin. "I don't know, honey. I just don't know." Annie wiped her face and shook her head quickly as if to erase the thought.

"Now let's stop all this sad talk and find some cute school clothes for you."

When they returned home, the house was stuffy and still. Annie sent Katrina to put away the shopping bags while she opened windows around the house.

Katrina had returned to find her mother sitting at the kitchen table, crying. The breeze from the open window blew her hair into an unruly nest around her head. Her hand trembled as she held a sheet of crumpled stationery. Annie didn't notice when her daughter came into the room. Katrina walked behind her mother's chair to read the note. She saw the last couple of lines before Annie crumpled the page and rose to throw it into the garbage can. *I feel like the walls are closing in on me. I have to go away for a while. Love, Earl.*

Annie told Katrina that her father was going away on a business trip and sent her daughter to stay with family in Indiana for a while. She said she thought Katrina should spend some time with her cousins before the end of the summer.

When Katrina got back, it was the hottest day of August. The kitchen was painted lemon yellow. And her parents were getting a divorce.

Now Katrina looked at the yellow walls and sipped lemonade from the same glass she'd given Annie as a Mother's Day gift ten years ago. She felt almost like a kid again, protected and yearning for answers that were shadowy and out of reach.

"So, tell me all about it." Annie settled into the chair across from Katrina.

She felt uncomfortable during these interrogatory sessions with her mother. She craved privacy, even as a child, and that was the one thing her mother was unable to give her. Annie wanted to know everything about her daughter, and she wasn't afraid to ask. When Katrina was fourteen, her mother had quizzed her about yeast infections in the cosmetics aisle at the supermarket, embarrassing her daughter so badly that she refused to go shopping with Annie for a month afterward and walked everywhere she needed to go.

"Tell you about what?"

Annie cocked her head to one side. "You're going to make this difficult, huh? Tell me about Patrick," Annie said impatiently.

"He's back. What else is there to say?" Katrina picked up a magazine off the coffee table to avoid meeting Annie's insistent gaze. Pretending that *The Ladies Home Journal* was the most interesting piece of literature she'd ever seen, she flipped the pages with great concentration.

Annie set her lemonade down on the glass coffee table top. The cup knocked against an ashtray and left a wet smudge on the spotless surface. No coaster. Katrina glanced around the spotless living room and braced herself. When Annie temporarily suspended her lifelong interest in avoiding rings on her tables and gave Katrina her undivided attention, there was bound to be a problem.

"Katrina Louise Larson, let's be serious. I know that Patrick's back. I know he's been gone five years. I know he was your best friend. I know how you felt when he left," Annie shot out. "Now stop reading that damned magazine and talk to me!"

Katrina held up her palms and shrugged. "Okay, okay, I'm sorry. God!"

"First you stay away for months, then you don't even want to talk to your own mother." Annie continued to fuss.

"Mom, Patrick is doing great. Wonderful. He's been traveling all over the world, and now he's back."

Annie eyed Katrina suspiciously. "Why did he leave so suddenly in the first place? I thought you and he were going to get an apartment together in Milwaukee, then one day he was just gone, and you never said much about it."

Katrina wondered if she could explain without telling her mother how in love she was with Patrick. It wasn't that she was ashamed—she just didn't want to jinx it.

"Mom, I don't know, really."

"Did you ask?"

"Can I finish?"

"Don't get smart with me."

"I'm sorry, I'm sorry. I guess he just wanted to travel, to

see the world, with some college friends."

"What friends?"

"I don't know them except from hearing him talk about them when we were in school. A guy named Jamie, I think, and a few other people."

"Jamie? That sounds pretty girlish."

"Mother, do you want me to tell you what I know or not?"

Annie waved a hand dismissively. She lifted her glass off the table, wiping away the dampness underneath with her fingertips. She leaned back and sighed. "So, he's back. How are you two getting along?"

Katrina shifted in her seat and remembered her attempt to kick Patrick off the bed. No way could she tell her mother how uncertain she felt, how her happiness to have Patrick back was tempered by doubt and worry. It would be one more thing for Annie to nag her about, and she didn't think she could face much more nagging right now.

"It's great to have him back. I really missed him."

A lot, she thought, remembering their first night together. She still wasn't used to being Patrick's lover. It was an unfamiliar sensation, having a dream as old as her adolescence become real. She was lost in thinking of her reunion with Patrick and didn't notice her mother's raised eyebrows.

"Do you love him?"

"Huh? Of course I love him. He's been my best friend forever."

Annie smiled gently at her daughter. "Katrina. Do you love him?"

Katrina looked around the room, searching for a reason not to answer. It was too new. It wasn't time to talk about this with her mother or anyone else. Not yet. But it was obvious her mother already knew.

"Yes. I love him," she said quietly. "And no, I don't know

if he's staying. So can we please talk about something else?"

"Sure. How's his dried-up old mother and his wimpy father?"

Katrina laughed. "His father's not exactly wimpy. He's just quiet."

"Uh-huh. That old woman probably sewed his lips shut a long time ago. So I guess the old bat's still alive?"

"Mom!"

Annie and Katrina looked at each other and burst into laughter.

Annie finally controlled herself and sniffed the air. "I think the chicken's ready. Are you hungry?" She rose and held her hand out to Katrina.

"Starving."

Sitting in front of the TV after dinner, Katrina watched her mother knit a pumpkin-colored scarf. Annie still wore her long black hair loose, and it gleamed under the lamplight. She wasn't old—fifty wasn't old—and Katrina thought her mother was surely too young to be sitting, knitting, with only her adult daughter for company.

"Mom, don't you ever get lonely up here?"

"Lonely?"

"I mean, living in a different city. At least in Milwaukee you had all your old friends and Aunt Lacey and Uncle Kenneth to keep you company."

Annie held up the half-finished scarf to the light.

"I've made new friends. I have my job at the school, and I meet the girls from the cultural center for lunch once a week."

"What about Lacey and Kenneth?"

"What about them? They're still your father's brother and sister-in-law. And as far as I'm concerned, they're still family even though your father and I aren't together anymore."

Annie bit off a length of yarn and began knitting another row. "Anyway, why are you so worried about me? I like Madison. I get more peace and quiet here."

The quiet in her mother's house felt melancholy to Katrina, not peaceful. She wondered how long it had been since her mother had a close friend to spend time with. How long had it been since her mother had a boyfriend? Katrina couldn't remember anyone serious. When she was a kid, her mother's male friends would come around occasionally, trying desperately to impress Katrina. But she figured they must have tried too hard—or not hard enough—to impress Annie, because none of them ever stayed over, and none of them lasted more than a month or two.

"But don't you miss them?"

"Who?"

"Aunt Lacey and Uncle Ken," she persisted.

"Katrina, they're not dead. They're less than two hours away."

"You used to see them every day."

"So?"

"So, I would think you might miss them." Katrina leaned forward in her seat. "Could you put down the scarf for a minute? I'm trying to make sure you're all right."

Annie set down her knitting and looked at Katrina sharply. "I'm fine."

Katrina rolled her eyes and searched around her feet for her purse. She figured she should leave now before the evening went completely wrong and they both felt sorry they'd even bothered.

"Okay, Mom. I'm sorry. I wasn't trying to hassle you. I'm going to go home now." She was frustrated with the double standard that allowed her mother to interrogate but Katrina wasn't afforded the same latitude. She stood up.

"Honey, don't leave yet."

"Why? You won't talk to me." Katrina crossed her arms.

"God, where do you get this stubborn streak from?" Annie shook her head. "I don't miss Lacey and Ken, okay? They just remind me of your father."

Katrina softened and sat back down. "Dad's been gone for years, Mom. Long before you moved here."

"What's your point?"

"I don't really understand."

Annie sighed and took off her reading glasses. "Darling, after all those years I just couldn't take it anymore. Kenny was your father's younger brother. He spent his whole life following Earl around like he was a hero, and when he married Lacey, she just jumped right on that bandwagon. They love to talk about how great Earl is. But let me ask you this: When was the last time you heard from your father?"

Katrina thought for a moment. "I guess it was when he called me to congratulate me on my high school graduation."

Annie squinted. "Some fucking hero."

"Mom!"

"Oh, Katrina, really! I'm a grown woman. I can say fuck occasionally if it's called for. Anyway, that's not the point. The point is, Earl hasn't spoken to his daughter in ten years. You loved him so much! Believed every bedtime story he told you like it was the honest-to-God truth. Nobody could say a bad word about your daddy when you were little, not even as a joke, without you defending him. And now I'm supposed to listen to his brother and sister-in-law blather on about how great he is?"

Katrina blinked back tears as she looked around the room. This was the most her mother had ever said about her father since he left, and suddenly Katrina wasn't sure she wanted to talk about it. She'd gotten used to his not being around much when she was a kid and not at all during the past decade. Why start thinking about him now? Part of her would always be "Daddy's girl," waiting for him to come back and make whole-wheat pancakes, the only food he knew how to cook. That part of her needed to talk about her father.

"You never said much about Dad after he left," Katrina said, hesitant.

"I know. I didn't really have anything good to say when it first happened, so I didn't say anything at all. And then, once it didn't hurt so much, you seemed to be doing okay, so I didn't want to bring up bad memories."

"Mom, my father is a little more than an unpleasant memory."

"That came out wrong. I didn't mean that Earl was unimportant to you. I figured that you were okay since you did see him every so often when you were younger," Annie said.

"Well, the visits tapered off, and I kind of felt he wasn't that interested in me anymore." Katrina remembered the times she'd called him to talk about a volleyball game or an "A" she'd gotten on a geometry test. Sometimes whoever answered the phone said he wasn't home. Sometimes there would be no answer at all. Sometimes the operator's nasal voice said the phone number was disconnected. Eventually she had stopped calling.

Annie frowned. "No, Katrina, I don't think that was it. I can't imagine that a man who loved his daughter as much as Earl loved you would have suddenly lost interest."

Katrina just sat there. She wasn't sure she wanted to go where this conversation was leading, but she couldn't help herself.

"Did you ever talk to him after the divorce? Do you know

why he stopped coming around?" She wished she wasn't so eager for an answer.

Annie looked pained. "We talked a little, but it was always difficult, uncomfortable. Neither of us knew what to say to the other and he never talked about where he was or what he was doing, and to be honest, I didn't ask because I was afraid of the answers. But he always asked about you, Katrina."

"So when was the last time you heard from him?"

"Your high school graduation, hon. Same as you."

Katrina couldn't control the tears any longer. "Do you think he's all right?" Her voice quavered. Maybe it would somehow be easier to take if he wasn't all right, if he'd died soon after her 18th birthday, or if he were sick and he couldn't call.

Annie held out her arms and enveloped Katrina in a hug.

"I wish I knew what to tell you," she said, holding Katrina tight.

They separated after a long while, and Katrina saw that Annie had been crying, too. But she wiped her palms across her cheeks and looked at her daughter with a smile filled with sadness and hope.

"It's late, and you have a long drive ahead of you. Are you sure you don't want to stay the night?"

Katrina kissed her mother on the cheek and stood up again. "Actually, Mom, I think I'll head home tonight."

Annie nodded. "I understand."

Katrina found her purse and walked to the door.

"Drive safe, honey," Annie called as Katrina walked to her car.

She turned around and blew her mother a kiss. "Love you!"

Later that night, after she'd appeased her mother with a phone call and a promise to visit soon, Katrina called Patrick.

The phone rang about fifteen times before a groggy Mrs. Flannery growled into the receiver. Katrina hung up quickly, hoping the Flannerys didn't have Caller ID. As she wondered where Patrick was at 10:30 on a Monday night, Katrina heard a rustling near her front door.

She found Patrick waiting with a stack of books under one arm and a bag of potato chips under the other. The books teetered precariously in his grasp, and she smiled.

"Patrick, what are you doing?" She ushered him in. He dropped the books on the nearest end table. "I brought a bunch of books for us to choose from. I thought we'd each pick one, then summarize it for the other and read any passages that seemed particularly interesting."

Katrina glanced at the dusty books. "Where did you get those?"

"My mother's basement, of course."

"Are they hers?" She was dubious.

Patrick laughed. "Come on, you know my mother reads the local section of the newspaper, the TV Guide and the occasional Robin Cook thriller. I don't know whose these were, but they're ours now."

She walked over and hugged him. She was happy to see him, happy to let him take her mind off her father's whereabouts and her mother's loneliness. "It's a great idea, and I'm glad to see you."

He kissed the top of her head. "Now, pick out one of the steamy ones for me, and I'll act it out for you."

Later, Katrina lay on the sofa with her head on Patrick's chest while she slipped in and out of a restless sleep. She'd dozed off to the sound of Patrick reading "Hills Like White Elephants," his voice fading into a hypnotic whisper as she drifted. A Coltrane CD played softly in the background and she savored the tickle of his fingers in her hair. He shifted a bit, looking for the most comfortable spot, and his movement jarred Katrina awake. She looked up at him, rubbing her eyes and yawning.

"I missed the end of the story. Sorry. I had a really long day," she said.

He shrugged. "Now you'll never know how it ends."

"Oh, come on. You're not going to tell me?"

"I stopped reading when you fell asleep. But I'm sure they lived happily ever after. Isn't that how all bedtime stories end?" He glanced at the TV and reached for the remote. A sharp exhale of electricity, and the picture disappeared. "So what happened today that got you so tired?"

She rubbed her cheek on his T-shirt and pressed closer. "I told you I was going to my mom's house."

"Did something happen?" He gently pushed her off his chest and held her at arm's length, better to see the truth in her eyes. She read worry in his creased brow and looked away.

"It's nothing, really. We just ended up talking about my father."

Patrick frowned. "Your dad? Wow. You haven't mentioned him in years."

She sat back on the couch and picked at a loose thread on her shirt. She wasn't sure she wanted to bring back the knot that formed in her chest every time she talked about her father. She felt Patrick watching her and waiting.

"Do you want to talk about it?" He reached over and snapped the stray thread for her. She looked up, wishing she hadn't fallen asleep during Hemingway, wishing her father could have stayed buried in her heart.

"I don't know. The whole thing with my mom brought up all these ancient feelings."

"Like wondering where he is."

"Like wondering if he's ever coming back." *I will not cry,* she told herself. *I will not cry*. She didn't think she could stand it if Patrick felt sorry for her. But the set of his mouth was thoughtful, not pitying.

"Maybe it's better if you just talk about it?" He framed this as a question, leaving it up to her.

"Why? How is it better? I can tell you one thing—I feel way worse today after talking about him than I did yesterday while still pretending to ignore it for ten years." Her voice rose, and she instantly felt sorry for lashing out.

But he simply nodded. "Sometimes I think all that 'express your feelings, deal with your issues' stuff is bullshit. You have to do whatever it takes to get through the day." He smoothed her hair off her face.

She lay back down next to him, shifting around to find the place where their bodies molded perfectly.

"I don't want to spend the rest of my life waiting for someone who must not care anymore," she said. In the silence she could hear the buts. *But* he's your father. *But* maybe he couldn't be here for some reason. *But* you love him.

Patrick didn't say anything. He hugged her tightly and held on when she could no longer keep her tears inside.

"You don't have to talk about him. Just be happy." After his shirt was wet with her tears, she slipped into an exhausted slumber. She felt his small movement and the whisper of pages as he picked up the book to read and drowsily wondered if he would finish the story.

Chapter 5

Katrina dialed Chrissy's number feeling tense and guilty. They hadn't talked in the three weeks since Patrick had returned; she hadn't even told Chrissy about it. She'd left a message the day they were supposed to meet, the day after Patrick came back, saying something had come up and she'd avoided returning Chrissy's messages until nearly a month passed. She felt bad about keeping secrets, and she hoped Chrissy would forgive her at some point before they were confined to an old-age home. She and Chrissy had shared a lot in college, but Katrina hadn't talked very much about Patrick. And while Katrina and Patrick were apart, Chrissy was her best friend. Even in college, Katrina didn't tell Patrick when she lost her virginity her sophomore year; Chrissy had been there to pick up the pieces.

She had met her first lover at a sorority party. Chrissy was pledging Delta Psi Omega and wanted Katrina to, too, so she dragged her to one of their mixers. Katrina refused to pledge, and she agreed to go only because Chrissy threatened to play Led Zeppelin in their dorm room all night if she didn't.

She had seen him around campus. He was hard to miss—six-foot-four, skin the color of warm caramel, hazel-green eyes, dreadlocks down his back. She'd nodded to him a couple of times at Black Student Association meetings. They had a class together, intermediate French. But they had never talked until he tapped her on the shoulder at the Delta Psi Omega fall party. She stood alone near a large bay window while Chrissy schmoozed. Katrina felt out of place in the big old house that had been rented especially for this night. The main room was cavernous, lit dimly by antique chandeliers, footsteps echoing on the plank wood floors. Flowers dotted the room along with tables piled with finger foods and drinks and portraits of the rich and dead on the walls.

"Hi. You're Katrina, right?"

She turned around, startled. "Yeah. Hi." She couldn't think of anything cool to say, and she wondered how he knew her name.

"My name is Kevin."

"Nice to meet you."

He glanced around the room. He had a way of looking people up and down for just a beat too long, as if he needed the extra time to categorize each person. "I don't know too many of these people. How did you end up here?" His smile was wry and confident.

"My roommate Chrissy blackmailed me." She felt unsure of herself, and she was out of her element among sorority girls and their friends. Any minute she was afraid she might laugh too loud or say the wrong thing, and those kinds of mistakes could be deadly with this crowd. She didn't care so much about embarrassing herself, but Chrissy loved this sorority stuff and Katrina didn't want to ruin it for her.

"Blackmailed you with what?" The crowd was thickening and people pressed against her from all sides. Kevin pressed closer, too, and she couldn't tell whether he was deliberately leaning against her breast. Deliberate or not, she wasn't sure if she was annoyed or happy about it.

"Led Zeppelin. Small room. All night."

He winced and laughed. "I think you made the right choice."

"Me, too. What about you?" She glanced at the crowd. All

of the guys could have been J. Crew models, with their casually rumpled khakis and straight blondish hair. She looked pointedly at Kevin's dreads. "It doesn't exactly seem like your type of party."

He nodded. "I write for the school paper, and I'm doing a story on the differences between white and black sororities. Figured I should do some research."

She smiled. "Looks like you've come to the right place."

They stood there for a while. She tried to think of something else to say, playing with a strand of her hair and looking around the room. It always seemed so easy for people like Chrissy, who was at the opposite end of the room laughing conspiratorially with another future Delta. Chrissy saw Katrina watching her and waved.

"How did you know my name?" she finally asked.

"I see you around. I'm a reporter. It's my job to notice people." He switched gears. "Hey, can I get you a drink?"

She didn't drink much. She hated the taste of beer, wine gave her a headache and brown liquor made her queasy. But the grandfather clock had just chimed ten, and she knew Chrissy wouldn't want to leave before two. She shrugged. "Sure."

They found a spot on a loveseat near the window and spent the rest of the night drinking punch laced with vodka and making fun of people who walked by.

"You are so beautiful," Kevin whispered during a lull. His eyes were half-closed and he leaned close so his breath tickled the spot on her neck just below her ear. She felt light-headed and dry-mouthed.

"Whatever, Kevin. You never said two words to me before tonight." It seemed important to challenge him, even though she didn't move away when his hand rested on her thigh.

"I was afraid of getting rejected. I mean, look at you." He looked down at her long legs encased in slim black jeans, her brown eyes set wide apart, her hair pulled up into a ponytail. "You're gorgeous."

She rolled her eyes and turned away. "Come on."

Kevin rested his palm against her cheek and turned her face toward him. "You. Are. Gorgeous." He kissed her lightly on the lips, tasting of vodka and lemon. "Want to get out of here?" he murmured.

She blinked slowly. She couldn't really think of a good reason not to go with him. She nodded and looked around for Chrissy to say good-bye.

Chrissy scowled when she noticed the glass in Katrina's hand. "You don't drink."

"It's a party. What's the big deal?" Katrina leaned against the wall and wished she could lie down.

Chrissy took the glass and sniffed it. "Whoa, this is strong. Where did you get it?"

"My friend. Kevin," she said.

Chrissy frowned and looked around. "Kevin who?" She scanned the crowd. Her eyes narrowed when she spotted him. "Do you even know him?" Chrissy held the glass away as Katrina reached for it.

"I do now."

Chrissy grabbed her wrist. "Don't do this. He's got a reputation around campus."

"So? He thinks I'm gorgeous." Her cheeks felt warm and a little numb at the same time.

"So do I. That doesn't mean he deserves to sleep with you." Chrissy paused. "What about Patrick?"

"What about him? For the thousandth time, he's not my boyfriend."

"Katrina, come on."

"See you later, Chrissy." She walked toward the door where Kevin stood waiting.

"Be careful!" Chrissy called after her.

Kevin's room was dark and musty. He wouldn't listen to her when she told him to go slowly. When she cried out from the pain, he shushed her. It was over in minutes. Her mouth tasted sour and her head pounded.

His parting words to her, mumbled while she quickly dressed, shamed her.

"You're not going to make this into some big thing, are you?"

Katrina had forced what she hoped was a derisive laugh. "Why would I?"

"It's good to be able to just hang out and have fun without it being a whole big deal."

She was sore and sticky. "Right. Just hanging out and having fun," she had said on her way out the door.

She cried in Chrissy's arms the next morning. Chrissy never said "I told you so." She just brushed Katrina's hair and listened.

They had remained friends. Chrissy had moved to Milwaukee after college, taking a job as a social worker for people with "real problems." Chrissy scoffed when Katrina suggested that even the problems of white, middle-class people in her northern Wisconsin neighborhood were real.

Now, waiting for Chrissy to answer, she hoped her friend would be as understanding as she had been when they were in college.

"I am so pissed at you!" Chrissy spat as soon as she heard Katrina's voice.

"Chrissy, I know. Just give me a chance to explain."

"Whatever, Katrina. I haven't heard from you in weeks,

and now you suddenly want to have lunch? This is really no way to treat me, you know." Katrina wished she could make up in person instead of over the phone.

"Will you at least meet me for coffee so I can tell you what's been going on?"

"What do you mean? Something's going on?" The curiosity in Chrissy's voice belied her irritation.

"You'll never know unless you meet me for coffee. Now."

"Well, all right, but I'm still pissed."

She smiled. "See you at The Ground Floor in about twenty minutes."

Katrina arrived early. The cool air blowing from the ceiling fans was a welcome relief from the Indian summer that had gripped Milwaukee like a jealous lover. She looked around the coffee shop. Abstract watercolor paintings covered the walls of the large, airy room, and the sharp scent of vanilla beans, cocoa and expensive coffee swirled in the air. The Ground Floor was filled with Saturday-afternoon shoppers taking a break, paper shopping bags at their feet. Katrina caught snippets of their conversations. A mother told her son she was never going to pay a hundred dollars for sneakers, and that was that. A young woman giggled at a joke told by her older male companion while she played with the sparkling diamond ring on her finger. A girl, her face covered in acne, sat sullenly at a table alone. School had just started, and Katrina could smell fall in the air. She could see it in the resigned expressions of the children scattered throughout the restaurant. It was the time for a fresh start, or at least a new twist on the familiar.

A teenaged waitress who cracked gum between her teeth pointed Katrina toward an empty booth next to a window. She ordered an iced cappuccino and wondered how Chrissy would react to the news that Patrick was back in town.

Chrissy had been there when Katrina pined silently over him during college, and she'd been there when he dropped out of sight for five years. Somehow, she doubted that Chrissy was going to take the news well. Even though they'd never met, Chrissy wasn't exactly a Patrick fan. But if Chrissy could just get to know him, she might understand. She was halfway through her drink when Chrissy breezed in. "You're late."

Chrissy smiled and reached down to hug Katrina. "So, the last time I talked to you it was August. Neither of us could believe how fast the summer was going. It is now September. I think we're even."

They kissed cheeks, and all was forgiven.

Chrissy ordered a double espresso and settled in. "So. Tell me what's been so engrossing that you couldn't be bothered to call me."

Katrina stirred the dregs in her cup. She didn't know where to begin.

"Katrina, please! I dragged my butt down here. The least you could do is talk."

"You live, like, three minutes away."

"Look, I have errands to run, laundry to do and hair to wash on this fine Saturday afternoon. Instead, I'm sitting here listening to you hem and haw. Now, what is it?" Chrissy tossed her long blond hair back and narrowed her eyes at Katrina.

Chrissy had a way of forcing her to examine truths she would prefer to keep hidden under layers of smiles, shrugs and evasions. Under her friend's insistent gaze, she simply blurted out the news.

"Patrick is back."

They sat watching each other.

Chrissy finally broke the silence. "He's back? Back from where?"

Katrina shifted in her seat and ran her fingers through her curls. "Traveling. In Asia, Australia, Europe. All over."

"With whom?"

Katrina shrugged, and Chrissy became impatient. "Why don't you start from the beginning."

Katrina told Chrissy about Patrick's sudden return, leaving out the part about the sex. She hoped Chrissy wouldn't catch on—at least, not right away. She wasn't sure how she'd explain it so she didn't sound weak and needy.

Chrissy played with her napkin and ordered another coffee while Katrina talked.

"Chrissy, it's so good to have him back. It was like a part of me was missing, you know?"

Chrissy looked at her closely, and Katrina knew she'd given herself away.

"So, for the past few weeks you have been having sex with Patrick even though you have no idea where he has been for the last five years."

"He was traveling. Who needs details?"

Chrissy shook her head. "I need details, and you should, too." She raised her eyebrows. "I notice you didn't deny the sex and love part."

Katrina shrugged. Her eyes pleaded for understanding. She needed someone on her side, someone who would be happy for her.

"I guess I finally have to admit that I've always loved Patrick—I've always been in love with him."

"Well, it only took you five years to admit it to me. Not bad," Chrissy laughed. But she didn't let Katrina off the hook.

"Seriously, is he staying?"

Katrina looked down at the table. She wanted to admit that she thought Patrick was leaving out some parts of his traveling stories, that she wondered if there was a woman or women somewhere in the picture. She didn't want to say how much she wanted to bury her doubts and just be happy.

"I don't know."

"Well, what does he say?"

"Not much. He's hanging out with his parents a lot."

Katrina winced at Chrissy's frown. Her disapproval was palpable. "We're having so much fun. I don't want to ruin it." Katrina felt her cheeks turn hot with embarrassment colored by anger. She wasn't sure whom she was angry at. "I'm not saying he just gets to do whatever he wants while I sit around and swoon."

"I'm glad you're not saying that."

"I'm not! I've just been enjoying the past month and trying not to think about the future."

Chrissy softened. "I understand that, believe me. But the future has a way of sneaking up on you, you know?"

She was relieved that Chrissy wasn't too hard on her. She looked around for a waitress and held up her cup to ask for another cappuccino.

"Don't worry, C. Just be happy for me."

"I am happy for you, honey. But I don't want you to get hurt."

"I know. And I love you for it." She glanced at her watch. "Damn—how can it be five o'clock already? I promised Patrick I'd meet him for a movie tonight. And I didn't even get a chance to ask about Rick." She made a move to get up and ask for her coffee to go.

Chrissy grabbed her arm playfully. "Well, you're just going to have to call him and tell him you can't make it. He's had you all to himself, and I haven't even begun to catch you up on my life. I do have a life, you know, even if it doesn't have a mysterious Patrick-like figure in it," Chrissy teased.

"I'd love to meet Patrick, finally, but tonight, I think you owe me some quality time."

Katrina shook her head. She knew it was important not to let Patrick—or any man—take over her life, yet he was doing just that.

"Oh, God, I'm being so self-centered. Don't hate me."

"Make it up to me by going out with me tonight," Chrissy smiled.

Katrina laughed. "It's impossible to say no to you, isn't it?"

"It's part of my charm."

Katrina bobbed her head to the thumping beat of electronica and looked around Vinyl, which was, according to Chrissy, the hottest club in Milwaukee. Chrissy was always making declarations like that: CK One was the hottest cologne for men, silver was the hottest accessory, red was the hottest color for fall. Katrina tended to ignore these trendy pronouncements, but sometimes, like tonight, Chrissy insisted on showing her what she was missing.

The walls of the club were painted black and covered with murals of stick figures and diamonds in fluorescent hues. The floor was covered in glitter that stuck to the skin, making the dancers flash like silvery ghosts. Adolescent-looking girls wore tiny skirts and nearly invisible tops, pressing their flesh suggestively against older men wearing vests with no shirts underneath.

The DJ sat in his soundproof booth high above the dancers, carefully examining the records to choose the perfect sound. Bored bartenders sloshed drinks along the futuristic stainless steel bar. A mist of sweet smelling marijuana smoke clouded the room, distorting faces and making Katrina feel like she was watching a slow motion art film where the characters quoted obscure French poetry and spoke in mysterious half-phrases. She sniffed the air and fleetingly wished she were a different, more relaxed kind of person who would ask for a hit.

Instead, she sipped her vodka tonic and turned to Chrissy. "This place makes me feel old," she shouted in her ear.

"What?" Chrissy's eyes were closed as she moved her sinewy body to the music. She wore tight, dark blue jeans and a black halter that clearly outlined her small breasts and pointed nipples. With her golden hair swept up, Chrissy looked amazing, and Katrina felt large and frumpy next to her. The top of Chrissy's head came up to Katrina's shoulders, and her petite frame was perfectly proportioned. Katrina felt overdressed in her black mini-dress and chunky heels. Her legs seemed too long, her breasts too round, her skin too dark, her hair too curly and wild in comparison with Chrissy's elegant sensuality.

"I said, this place makes me feel old. And you make me feel like a gigantic slob."

Chrissy opened her eyes and smirked.

"We're only 27! And I'd kill to be tall, curvaceous and exotic looking like you. I'm shaped like a boy, for Chrissakes. Haven't you noticed that every guy in here is looking at you?"

Katrina glanced around in time to meet the eyes of one of the bartenders. He winked at her and mouthed something she didn't catch. She looked away quickly.

"I guess it's just been so long since I've been to a club. Look at all these sixteen-year-old girls prancing around trying to pass for twenty-one."

Chrissy laughed. "I know. Part of the fun of going to clubs is making fun of them and being happy you're not sixteen anymore."

They watched as a voluptuous brunette in a green tube top

and tight white capri pants approached the bartender who'd winked at Katrina. She leaned over the bar, showing mounds of tanned cleavage, and whispered into his ear.

"I wish I could hear what Miss Tits on Display is saying to your boyfriend over there," Chrissy said. They watched as the bartender pulled away and shook his head.

"Ah, another underage nymphet goes without a banana daiquiri," Katrina laughed. She turned to Chrissy. "Let's have one more drink, then get out of here," she said.

The opening bars to Nine Inch Nails' "Closer" came blasting over the speakers.

"Only if you get the drinks—I'm going to dance!" Chrissy called back on her way to the dance floor.

Katrina hoped she wouldn't get Mr. Winky, but as she walked up to the bar, he was waiting for her.

"Hey, gorgeous, what can I do for you?" He was confident and knowing, never doubting for a second that she'd be impressed with his smug charisma. He didn't just think he was good-looking—he knew it. He moved with a swagger that came precariously close to being a caricature of a "cool bartender guy at a trendy club." But Katrina looked past his excessively familiar manner and his aggressive charm to his face, which had an asymmetry that was disconcerting. His nose was a little crooked, and his smile was crooked, too, but in an almost endearing way.

"So what'll it be, darlin'?"

Katrina rolled her eyes. "You can get me two vodka tonics. Absolut."

He grinned. "Anything else, sweet thing?"

"Yeah. You can stop being a cheeseball, and promise never to call me 'sweet thing' again."

Katrina expected him to get mad, but instead he laughed. She noticed the way his mahogany skin gleamed against the white of his button-down shirt. His hair was close cropped, and his ear was pierced, but he didn't wear an earring. He wasn't bad looking, she decided. Just a little unusual. When he turned to look for the bottle of Absolut behind the cheap stuff they fed to the kids, Katrina was surprised: was it possible to look better than this in jeans?

"Here's your drinks. Oh, and I'm sorry about that earlier thing—hitting on girls, it's a part of the job. Sometimes I forget how to act normal." He smiled apologetically.

"Occupational hazard. I understand." She took both drinks and started to walk away.

"Hey, wait a second." She turned around.

"My name is Linc Davis. I thought maybe you might want to hang out sometime?"

"Linc?"

"Got it. Short for Lincoln."

"Of course. Linc, I have a boyfriend, but thanks anyway."

He shrugged. "Maybe I'll see you around, then?"

"Maybe. Nice meeting you, Linc." She walked back to Chrissy, whose face was covered in a fine sheen from dancing.

"You and your bartender friend sure seemed cozy," she said, taking her drink.

"He called me 'sweet thing,' but he apologized after I called him a cheeseball," Katrina reported, sipping her drink. She couldn't stop thinking about the way he'd looked at her, as if he were already imagining her sliding around in his king-sized bed. Tacky, she thought, shaking her head and sipping the drink that tasted more like Absolut than tonic. But she wondered what he'd mouthed to her when he winked at her earlier.

"He may be corny, but he makes a damn good vodka tonic," Chrissy said.

Katrina felt guilty for thinking about Linc. Patrick was back. They were lovers. Why think about this bartender who wore his sexuality like too much cologne?

"Drink up. I'm getting bored with this place."

Chrissy downed her drink in seconds, and Katrina followed suit, wiping an errant drop of liquid from her chin.

"Then by all means, let's go."

As they walked to the exit, Katrina glanced back toward the bar. She met Linc's eyes as they followed her out the door.

Chrissy ended up at Katrina's apartment, where they spread out a post-club snack of soda, popcorn, Twinkies and beef jerky on the living room floor.

"Thank God 7-Eleven stays open twenty-four hours," Chrissy said through a mouthful of popcorn.

Katrina nodded and broke open a beef jerky.

"Ugh. How can you eat that? I'd weigh about a million pounds if I ate that stuff."

Katrina shrugged and shoved the entire stick into her mouth.

"It's one of the advantages of being tall—I can eat anything without gaining much weight," Katrina said, swallowing with satisfaction. "Plus, this is a celebration, so have a Twinkie!"

Chrissy giggled. "Okay, but what are we celebrating?"

Katrina sipped her Coke and considered. "We're celebrating Patrick's coming home, and your new boyfriend. Rick."

"Here's to Patrick and Rick."

They both sipped from their bottles, then lay back on the carpet and closed her eyes. "So tell me what Rick's like."

Chrissy, finishing her second Twinkie, leaned down on

one elbow and stared off into space, thinking.

Katrina looked up in surprise. She'd never known Chrissy to be at a loss for words over a man. Her usual philosophy was to use and leave men before they could do the same.

"I don't know how to describe him. He's just so . . ."

"Wonderful? Handsome? Rich?" Katrina offered.

Chrissy shook her head. "I think the word I was looking for is generous."

"So he *is* wealthy?"

"Oh, God, no. I mean, he teaches art at the community college. He just cares so much, about painting, about his students. He takes it so personally if one of them can't quite get it. He teaches way more classes than he has to and not because of the money. He just feels responsible for his students," she said dreamily.

"So he's like you at the clinic, really into helping people?"

Chrissy considered this. "It's not the same. I want to help people, but there are plenty of days I think my dad is right, that I should just go to law school or business school and get a "real" job. And I definitely don't love all the people who come in the clinic." She stopped and sighed. "But Rick, he feels an almost brotherly love for those students, even though most of them aren't serious artists. Most of them just want to take an easy class. But he still looks forward to teaching them every day. He has a generous heart."

Katrina felt a little sad, a little jealous, but talked herself out of comparing Rick to Patrick. Patrick loved her, and things were different between them, anyway. They'd known each other since they were kids, while Chrissy was still caught up in the early giddiness of a relationship when the other person seems infallible. She wanted to be happy for Chrissy, and she was.

"And, I assume, he's gorgeous, too, on top of all that. I

know your type!" Chrissy relaxed and lay back on the carpet next to Katrina.

"He's beautiful to me."

"So do your parents know about Rick? Do they know he's Puerto Rican?"

"No, and I'm not planning on telling them anytime soon."

"But if it's that special, don't you want to share it with them?"

"It's so new. And I'm just afraid that if I talk about him they'll find a way to spoil this for me, you know?"

Katrina knew exactly what she meant. It was how she felt when her mother grilled her about Patrick. It was how she felt when Chrissy demanded details about what he'd been doing during those years. She finally had Patrick back. She didn't want to worry about the past or the future and spoil what they had right now.

Chrissy reached for another soda and spilled it on the carpet as she tried to drink while lying down. She shrugged and licked the sides of the bottle to try and salvage what she could.

"Speaking of parents, how's Annie?"

"Oh, the same. Still fussing at me every chance she gets. But it's weird, the last time I was there she was talking about my father." Katrina was immediately sorry that she'd brought it up.

Chrissy sat up and took a swig of soda. "Your father? You've never told me much about him."

She shrugged. She had no intention of getting into all that again. Not after drinking vodka all night. Not after ten years of trying to forget it. "Yeah, and I've never talked to my mom about him, either. Until the other day."

Chrissy poked Katrina in the shoulder. "What did she say? You haven't seen him since, what, high school?"

She wished she could think of an easy way to get Chrissy to

forget about her father, to forget the whole thing. "Yeah. Mom said she doesn't know where he is or anything. Whatever. It's no big deal."

Chrissy was not deterred. "Do you think he'll ever come back?"

"Who knows? I doubt it. It's been so long. Why bother at this point?"

"What would you do if he did show up?" Chrissy's voice was growing faint and sleepy. She set down her bottle and stretched out again.

"Oh, Chris, I don't know." Katrina yawned loudly, partly because she was tired and partly to end the conversation. "Hey, I was thinking, maybe we should have a dinner party or something, so I can meet Rick and you can finally meet Patrick."

"Good idea, darlin'. Now, I'm exhausted, so can I sleep here?"

"You know you don't even have to ask."

Katrina pulled herself up from the floor and helped Chrissy up. They dragged themselves into the hallway, where Katrina handed Chrissy a blanket and a pillow, pointing her toward the extra bedroom. Groggy, Katrina kissed her friend on the forehead before turning toward her own bedroom.

"Good night, Chris."

" 'Night, Katrina."

Chapter 6

Katrina sat naked and cross-legged on Patrick's new queen-sized bed, feeling the cool breeze from the open window dry her damp skin. It was late September, and Milwaukee was starting to settle into the gentle repose of a midwestern fall. After the unnatural heat of the extended summer, the chilled air would be a relief for a few weeks until it turned into frost and ice that required boots and parkas. For now, autumn soothed Katrina's flushed skin, and she breathed deeply to fill her lungs with its sweetness.

Patrick's room at the Flannerys' was different than it had been, with color-coordinated accessories that he would have scoffed at when they were kids. As she ran her fingers along the light-blue duvet cover, she wondered whether Mrs. Flannery or Patrick had made the changes.

He was downstairs rattling around in the kitchen, and Katrina looked around the room for the first time since he had called her in a whirl of covert excitement, saying his parents would be out for hours at some church fund-raiser. Intrigued and amused by the thought of having pseudo-adolescent sex in Mrs. Flannery's home, she had rushed over. She had been planning to call Patrick anyway to tell him about the party she and Chrissy were planning. She hadn't had a chance to talk to Patrick about it. Patrick didn't love parties, but he'd been willing to hang out with his old buddies from Regis and she was sure he'd be excited to meet her friends.

Now, an hour after they'd fallen into each other's arms

laughing and kissing, she noticed the differences in Patrick's old room. The posters of Bo Jackson holding a football in one hand and a baseball bat in the other had been replaced by black and white photos set in thick black frames. She recognized Barcelona and Berlin, although she'd never left the United States. Another photo showed a tiny, long-haired Korean girl eating some sort of meat stuffed in lettuce. Evidence of his travels, she thought, wondering who had taken the photos.

Katrina glanced around for what had been Patrick's most prized possession as a teenager: an autographed picture of Michael Jordan, obtained during the days when the Bulls were fallible and Jordan had hair. It used to stand in the center of Patrick's dresser in a gaudy gold frame, much to his mother's chagrin. But it was gone now, and its absence made Katrina strangely uncomfortable. She missed that Michael Jordan picture.

"Okay, which do you want, a hot dog, or a tuna sandwich?" Patrick entered the room wearing just a pair of boxers and balancing a tray filled with sandwiches, chips, soda and cookies. Katrina watched him maneuver around the bed, his black hair curling close to his scalp, still damp with sweat. She felt her stomach tighten with fleeting desire and worry.

"Tuna." She scooted over on the bed to make room for him as he handed her the sandwich. "Want to hear about the party Chrissy and I are planning?" She made her voice cheerful and pleasant.

"Party? What's the occasion?" he mumbled through a mouthful of Pringles.

"No occasion. Chrissy has this new boyfriend that I'm dying to meet, plus, you and she haven't met yet, so we figured it would be nice to have a little get-together." Katrina picked at her food, waiting for him to answer. He was very involved in picking the pickles off his hot dog, and she was annoyed. "Patrick?" He looked up innocently, as if he weren't using the pickles to stall. As if she didn't realize that if he hadn't wanted pickles, he wouldn't have put them on the hot dog in the first place.

"Yeah, it sounds fine. Maybe I'll go."

Maybe? She grabbed his discarded pickles and munched on them, trying to bury her annoyance in a large bite of tuna on rye. She swallowed and decided that she would either have to change the subject or get into a big fight over the word *maybe*.

"Hey, what happened to your Michael Jordan picture?"

"I took it with me while I traveled. Mom sent it to me before we left the States."

"But where is it now? I figured you'd have put it back in its place of honor," she said, trying to be casual while taking a sip of soda.

Patrick shrugged and finished off his first hot dog in two bites. "I guess it's still packed up. Who knows?"

Katrina told herself she was being silly. He was a grown man, after all. Why did she expect him to still care about some old photo of a retired basketball player?

"You've made a bunch of changes in here, I see. Matching duvet cover and curtains, for example."

"You got something against blue?" he teased.

"I'm just curious about the redecoration." Maybe this bed was a sign of stability?

"Well, I'm a little old for a Superman bedspread, so I bought them to spruce things up a bit in here."

"So, who took those photos on the walls?"

Patrick stopped eating and looked at Katrina impatiently and, she thought, a little warily.

"A friend. Jamie. Why all the questions?"

She shook her head dismissively. "I'm just interested in your life, Patrick. I don't know why it upsets you."

He looked away. "Sometimes I feel like you're cross-examining me, like there's something you're not saying."

"I'm not the one being all mysterious about the past five years."

He pushed the tray away and fumbled around on the floor for his T-shirt and jeans. "I told you about the places I lived, the sights I saw. That's not being 'mysterious.' " He turned his back to her while he rummaged for a sweater.

Katrina suddenly felt cold and pulled on her own shirt and underwear. "Patrick, sit down for a second."

He sat on the edge of the bed and waited for her to appease him. His expectant posture made her angry.

"Look, I just feel like you're not telling me everything."

"You're being paranoid," he said sharply. But then he relaxed against the headboard and covered Katrina's hand with his own.

"What about women? Love? You haven't said anything about that."

He looked at her intently. "I have talked about love, about how much I love you."

She saw the cajoling look in his eyes and knew what was coming. All he can think about is now, she thought, hearing his voice in her head. He doesn't want to talk about the past, he can't think about the future.

Before he could speak, she held up a hand to stop him. "It isn't fair. You're expecting a lot of me and not giving me much in return."

He softly touched her chin, guiding her face close to his. "Isn't it enough that I love you?" he whispered, brushing her lips with his. Involuntarily she closed her eyes, and pressed toward him. She wished she didn't love him. She wished she could pull away from the feel of his chest against hers. She wished she wasn't drowning in the vaguely musky scent of his skin.

No, she thought, not this time. It was not enough. She was tired of letting Patrick off easy, letting his kisses wipe away her doubts like warm hands on a frosty window. She was tired of not getting any answers. She pulled away from him and sat up, hoping he would notice her discomfort. He lay back on the bed and closed his eyes, and she felt worn out. She wished she were home in her own bed.

"So what about the party?" She knew it was bad timing, but there was no turning back.

"I said maybe, didn't I? You didn't even say where or when it's going to be."

His tone grated like gravel against her skin. Her body tensed, and Katrina felt the beginnings of a headache.

"We'll have it at Chrissy's place."

"Who's going to be there?"

She frowned. Since when was he so picky about whom he socialized with?

"Chrissy, Rick, me, you, and a bunch of other people. And I really want you to be there."

Patrick grunted. "I'm not that into parties."

"Don't you want to meet Chrissy?" She hated herself for pleading with him, begging him to care about this stupid party. She hated him for not simply saying yes.

He didn't answer. He just lay there as if he was dozing off, and Katrina wanted to slap his face to get his attention.

"So are you going or not?" Her voice was angry.

He turned to her and rubbed her leg invitingly.

"Can't we talk about this later? I'm not really in a talking mood right now," he murmured, leaning over and kissing the inside of her bare thigh.

She slid off the bed away from his lips and finished dressing. "Well, I *am* in the mood to talk about it. Everything is not about what *you* want and when *you* want it."

"Katrina?"

She slammed the door on her way out of the room, feeling unreasonable and furious. It was about the party, and then again it wasn't. She wanted him to go, yes, but maybe it wouldn't have mattered so much if it didn't feel he was keeping a part of himself separate from her. He was holding back, and refusing to go to the party was just one more way of doing that.

Later that night, Katrina curled up on her sofa to watch a rerun of *Weird Science* on TBS. She cried at the scene where the two nerds used a Barbie doll to create a woman. It reminded her of the time she and Patrick had gone to see the movie together in the theater. They'd taken the bus across town to the 4:30 matinee showing, and afterward they'd eaten thick slices of gooey cheese pizza at Rocky Rococo's. When Katrina's mother picked them up in her old red and white 1977 Thunderbird, she'd laughed as they sang the movie's theme song over and over. Before the car arrived at the Flannery home, Patrick and Katrina had agreed that the Barbie doll experiment was the best part of the movie.

But that was before they'd grown up, when they'd promised that nothing would ever change between them. Before she realized that almost everything *had* changed between them.

Wiping her eyes, she clicked off the television set and went to bed.

Katrina ignored the pounding on Chrissy's bathroom door as she puckered her lips in the mirror. She made this pouty, petulant model face whenever she looked closely in a mirror, and it bothered her. She thought it made her look vain, infatuated with her reflection. But the pucker was more disapproving than narcissistic.

She turned to look at her profile in the strapless red dress that skimmed the middle of her thighs and clung to her bottom. Too much? Chrissy had talked her into buying the dress even though it was almost November and they'd already seen the first frost. She felt too obvious in so much red—red dress, red lipstick. But Chrissy told her that the thing to do was to be bold and have fun. Get into the holiday spirit, she'd said. So Katrina did it, but now she was feeling chubby and uncomfortable.

She blotted her lips and applied more lipstick, wondering what Patrick was doing at that moment. In the three weeks since that night in his bedroom, he'd called during the first two weeks, and she'd talked to him, hoping that he would say something other than "sorry" and "try to understand." He still wasn't ready to talk about his personal life over the last five years—all he could do was talk about how beautiful Korea was and how he felt like he could live in Australia forever. She'd told him that a travelogue wasn't what she was looking for, and his reply had been silence. Then, yesterday, he'd left her a message saying he would come to the party "if it was such a big deal to her." His concession was nullified by the sharpness in his voice, and Katrina wasn't sure she even wanted him to come under duress. She wasn't interested in hearing any more excuses, and she didn't want to fight.

"Katrina! Get out here and help me with the food!" Chrissy pounded on the door again. "You look great."

She took one last critical look at herself in the mirror and opened the door. She smiled at Chrissy. "How did you know

I was in here wishing I hadn't let you talk me into buying this dress?"

"I know you. You look fantastic. Stop worrying. We've got a party to give!"

Chrissy's perkiness was infectious. "Is Rick here yet? I can't wait to meet him." Katrina tried to shake off the thoughts of Patrick as she walked arm in arm with Chrissy into the living room.

Chrissy made little money working as a social worker, but she managed to live in a small house in the upscale suburb of Shorewood. When she'd moved to Milwaukee, her parents had insisted on accompanying her on her apartment search. They were scandalized when they saw the neighborhoods she could afford, all of them in neighborhoods where the average skin color was considerably darker than a paper bag. Chrissy's father decided to supplement her meager salary with an allowance.

So, not only was Chrissy's house roomy and in a good neighborhood, it was furnished with expensive sisal rugs, Natuzzi leather furniture and the latest in high-end stereo equipment.

"Is this new?" Katrina asked, holding up a crystal vase.

Chrissy tossed back her hair and grinned. "Yeah. My mom wants me to come home for the holidays, so she's started the bribery."

"You have such a retarded relationship with your parents. You should go on Jerry Springer," Katrina teased.

"Oh, yeah, like you're one to talk about dysfunction. Just make sure you tape the show: 'Spoiled Daughters and Their Over-indulgent Parents.' "

"I'll set my VCR."

The doorbell rang, and they went to greet the first guest.

Katrina couldn't help but feel jealous as she watched

Chrissy wrap herself around her new boyfriend.

Chrissy wiped her pink lipstick from Rick's cheek with one hand and held his arm with the other. She turned to Katrina and smiled possessively. "Katrina, meet Rick."

Rick turned to face her and stuck out his hand, and she was surprised. She remembered what Chrissy had told her about Rick—"He's beautiful to me"—and she hadn't thought twice about it until now. She'd expected Rick to be glib and well-manicured, like the rest of Chrissy's boyfriends. Katrina had even imagined that he might be one of those rare fair-haired, fair-skinned Latinos, providing the right combination of all-American looks and exotic heritage. Chrissy usually liked to keep people off-balance with her choice of men, but she'd never been able to control her yearning for pretty boys.

Or that's what Katrina thought until she met Rick. His dark hair was long and pulled back into a misshapen ponytail. It looked as if he'd tried to slick it down, but errant curls escaped and stuck out at odd intervals. A thick beard covered most of his face, and Katrina noticed that one of his front teeth was chipped. He was short—not much taller than the diminutive Chrissy—and he wore baggy khakis with a rumpled shirt and tie.

But his light-brown eyes were intelligent and kind, and he smiled warmly at Katrina.

"I feel like I know you already from all Chrissy's talk," he said with a hint of an undulating Spanish accent.

He was not what she expected, but she could feel the generosity Chrissy had raved about in his hug and the way he seemed genuinely happy to meet her. She liked him immediately. "Hey, Rick! It's so good to finally meet you."

"This party was a great idea," he said, patting her arm amicably. "And, you look fantastic. Both of you."

Chrissy and Katrina smiled at each other.

"We do look fabulous, dahling," Chrissy drawled.

The doorbell rang again. "Okay, I'm putting you two to work. Rick, go put on some music. Something upbeat but not too loud. Katrina, can you check on the spinach-artichoke dip? I think I left it in the oven too long." Chrissy straightened her floor-length backless dress before opening the door.

Katrina and Rick looked at each other and laughed.

"I guess the workers better get to work," Rick joked, walking to the stereo.

"Yeah, you probably haven't seen Ms. Bossy when she doesn't get what she wants," she tossed back over her shoulder on her way into the kitchen.

The house was filled with the scent of baking bread, hors d'oeuvres, cigarettes and expensive perfume. Katrina tried to keep up with Chrissy's endless introductions, and during a bathroom run she fleetingly wondered how Chrissy knew twice as many people as she did when Katrina had grown up in this city.

The music was loud, and Rick had apparently ignored Chrissy's instructions to keep it mellow, because Katrina felt her body vibrate with each beat. Chrissy glowed in the mayhem as Katrina sat back and observed from her spot near the ficus tree. She held on to a weak rum drink made by one of Chrissy's friends from work, a mild-looking man with a bald spot and a tattoo of Donald Duck on his hip that he happily showed. Katrina felt like she should have known by his questionable choice of body art (if you *have* to go Disney, why Donald?) that he would make a substandard drink. But she sipped it periodically so as not to look anti-social or bored as she observed the action. She glanced at her watch. Patrick was an hour and a half late. She wondered when he would get there and wished she could pretend she didn't care.

Katrina found herself watching Rick throughout the evening. He had a way of touching Chrissy's shoulders gently to calm her when she passed him in a flurry of panic over a quickly depleting wine supply. At one point, Katrina noticed Rick and Chrissy hugging in a corner. They were so sweet together.

Katrina tried to be a good host and work the crowd for a while, but after more than an hour, she felt like she needed another drink. She felt like she needed Patrick. She hoped Chrissy was wrapped up enough not to notice her slipping into the bedroom to use the phone. She'd just call him to make sure he was on his way, she reasoned. She told herself that calling him wouldn't be a sign of weakness, of dependency, and she pretended to believe this as she drained her glass and turned toward the bedroom.

"Hi."

Just as she turned, she bumped into Linc, who was standing directly behind her, smiling. Katrina was surprised and confused, and she stood there looking at him for a moment. "Linc?"

"You remember. It's good to see you again," he said.

Katrina shook her head and squinted at him. "I remember. But what are you doing here?"

"What do you mean?"

He looked suspiciously close to laughing, which irritated Katrina.

"I suppose Chrissy invited you?"

"She did. I thought you'd be happy to see me, Katrina," he said, finally unable to keep from laughing.

"What's so funny?" She hated feeling like she was the butt of a joke she didn't get.

"Oh, I'm not laughing at you, exactly. If you could see the

expression on your face. You look like someone just pinched your ass on a crowded bus."

Now Katrina couldn't help laughing. "That bad?"

"That bad."

She recovered and tried to make up for snapping at him. She made a mental note to corner Chrissy, who was conveniently nowhere in sight.

"Can I get you a drink?" Just as she finished speaking, she noticed the glass he was holding in his left hand. "I'm sorry, you just caught me off-guard."

Katrina felt nervous but wasn't sure why. Everything felt off-kilter, surreal. She didn't know what was making her feel so weird around Linc, why she felt drawn to him. Maybe because he didn't give up easily. Most guys, when stung by her sharp tongue, backed off. She'd spent years perfecting her sarcasm to ward off even the most persistent suitors. Yet Linc simply laughed. She wasn't sure how to deal with it.

He held up his free hand and smiled. "Forget it, I understand. That dress is perfect, by the way. You look great."

She was buoyed by the compliment and smiled at him. Then, she guiltily remembered that she'd been about to call Patrick. She wasn't sure which was worse—feeling this spark of something for Linc, or calling Patrick. But then, Patrick was supposed to be here and he wasn't. She decided to try and get to the kitchen, eat something and clear her head. "Linc—"

He interrupted her. "Do you want to dance?" He made a little mock dancing motion to the beat of the thumping salsa music that rumbled through the room and looked at her hopefully.

What harm could one dance do? She took one last look at the bedroom door and shrugged. "Why not?"

Just then, the music changed to a slow, driving beat that

reminded Katrina of humid nights spent young and yearning, wishing for that perfect love and wondering if it existed. The music reminded her of phantom kisses just out of reach, so close they were almost real. She hesitated, thinking it might not be a good idea to dance to this particular song with Linc.

He held onto her hand and looked at her. "Please?" His voice was low. Katrina found that she didn't want to say no. She nodded slightly and followed him out into the cluster of couples.

They swayed together disjointedly at first, unsure of each other's rhythm. Katrina held herself at a distance, wary of dancing too close. She didn't even know Linc. He was just some bartender she'd met once at a club. But he was nice and funny, and he'd taken a chance, risking rejection.

Still, she held him apart, preferring the embarrassment of being clumsy to the alternative—this urge for someone new, someone who didn't know that her father was AWOL, didn't know that she hated her job, didn't know that she felt fat in red.

But Linc seemed to tire of being out of sync with her, and he pulled her tightly to him, ignoring her stiff arms. They stood still for a moment—she tense and resistant, he firm and insistent. Katrina finally relaxed into his arms and felt a pin-prick of desire for the unknown. It was a new feeling for her. She wanted to lay her head on his shoulder and surrender to the music. Instead, she spoke to distract Linc and herself.

"So, what made you come here?"

He looked down at her, eyebrows raised. "That's a silly question."

"I mean, isn't it kind of weird to come to a party to see two women you don't even know?"

"Weird? I don't know about that. I wanted to see you again."

"I told you I have a boyfriend, so why would you bother?"

He stopped dancing and pulled away slightly to look into her eyes. "I just had a good feeling about you and me."

She detached her arms from his waist. Was this some kind of line? "There's nothing going on between you and me."

"No?" He leaned closer to her face, and she was afraid he might kiss her. Panicking, she quickly tried to come up with a plan of action. Should she tell him off? Smile apologetically, shake her head and walk away? But he just stood there.

"I have a boyfriend, Linc." A boyfriend who'd said he was going to be here and wasn't, she thought.

"So where is this famous boyfriend of yours? What's his name again?"

"I never told you his name. It's Patrick. And he's not here."

"Obviously. The question is, *why* isn't he here? I bet if he'd known you were going to wear that red dress, he'd be here," Linc said playfully.

Hearing the question she'd been avoiding uttered out loud hit her like a sharp pinch on the soft skin of her arm. Suddenly everything felt wrong: Linc, the party, the dress. She didn't want to talk about Patrick with Linc. She backed away. "Thanks for the dance. I need to find Chrissy." She walked off and pretended she didn't hear him calling after her.

She slipped into the darkened bedroom, flicked on the light and was relieved to find herself alone. She looked at her watch. 11:37. Too late to call. She picked up the phone to dial the Flannerys' number anyway, wishing for the hundredth time that he didn't live with his parents. No answer. She didn't hear the door open behind her.

"Who are you calling?"

Katrina cringed at the sound of Chrissy's voice. Just what she didn't need—a lecture on how she shouldn't chase after

Patrick if he didn't want to be with her. She already knew all that. She composed her face into an expression of bland innocence before turning around.

"I was just checking my messages," she said with a bright smile.

Chrissy narrowed her eyes, closed the door behind her and folded her arms.

"Where's Patrick?"

Katrina cleared her throat. "He's not here yet."

Chrissy shook her head. "You were checking to see if he called, right?"

"No!" That part, at least, was true. Chrissy looked at her, disappointed, and she knew it was pointless to pretend.

"Okay, I called him."

"So what did he have to say?"

"Nothing. There was no answer."

Chrissy unfolded her arms. She walked over to sit next to Katrina on the bed. "Why are you doing this to yourself? He's just a jerk." Chrissy had a sympathetic look on her face that made Katrina want to scream. Poor, deluded Katrina, that look said.

"Chris, I know it's dumb. Please don't lecture me." It was enough that Katrina knew, deep down, that something was wrong, that Patrick should *want* to meet her friends. He should *want* to share everything about the past five years with her—not just his travel stories, but everything. He shouldn't have anything to hide. If he really loved her, he would tell her what was going on, and he wouldn't be a no-show tonight. She knew this. But she couldn't listen to Chrissy say it aloud.

"I'm not lecturing. I'm just not sure he's worth it."

Now Katrina felt as if she had to defend herself and Patrick. "You don't even know him—that's not fair."

Chrissy tilted her head to the side and frowned. "I wanted

to get to know him, tonight, but he's nowhere to be found."

"For someone who's not lecturing, you sound pretty sanctimonious." Katrina stopped herself. She didn't want to fight with Chrissy. "Let's just drop it, okay? He wasn't home, I didn't talk to him. Let's forget it."

"We could talk about why you sneaked away to call him," Chrissy said.

"Just let it go. And speaking of sneaky, I had no idea you and Linc were such good friends that you'd invite him to the party," she said, raising her eyebrows at Chrissy, who got up and walked over to the mirror.

"We don't socialize. I just happened to see him the other day, and I told him we were having a party," she said, smoothing down her pale hair and checking her teeth in the mirror.

Katrina laughed. "Now who's lying?"

Chrissy looked at Katrina in the reflection and smiled. "So? What difference does it make how he got here? I saw you dancing. You had this look on your face."

Katrina was alarmed. Had there been a look? And had Linc seen it? "What look?"

"A look like, hmmm-mmm!" Chrissy teased.

"What's that supposed to mean?"

"You tell me!"

Katrina shrugged. There couldn't have been a look. It was just a dance. "I don't even know what you're talking about."

"Oh, right." Finished correcting her image in the mirror, Chrissy turned around expectantly. "So what do you think of Rick?" Katrina saw how anxious Chrissy was for her opinion, and she knew for certain that this was more than a passing fancy, more than one of Chrissy's temporary passions that would fizzle in a month or so.

"He's wonderful. I feel really comfortable with him. And

he's got a great sense of humor." She wondered if she should mention the fact that he was so different from Chrissy's usual type. She hesitated.

"What? It's the looks, right?" Chrissy said.

"Well, he's not exactly what I expected." Katrina tried to be diplomatic. "I'm not saying he's unattractive. He's just not your usual type."

Chrissy walked closer to the bed and spoke conspiratorially. "I know. We met at a fund-raiser for the United Way that I went to for work, and at first I didn't even pay him any attention. But he came up to me, and we started talking, and I ended up spending the whole night laughing. And at the end of the night, he kissed me on the cheek and asked if he could see me again. By that time, I was hooked." Chrissy's face flushed while she spoke, and Katrina felt that now-familiar pang of envy in her chest.

"I've never seen you like this. So happy . . ." She didn't want to blurt out the *L* word and scare Chrissy away from these feelings.

"So in love." Chrissy finished the sentence for her.

Another first. Katrina had never heard Chrissy even joke about being in love with a man.

"Really?"

"Yeah, I really do think it's love. You know how I know? We haven't even had sex, and I still want to spend every minute I can with him."

Katrina smiled and held Chrissy's hand. "God, that's so nice." She rose and hugged her friend, remembering when her feelings for Patrick had been that pure. It seemed like such a long time ago.

They separated, and Katrina went to straighten her dress and pick at her hair in the mirror. Looking at herself, she wondered where Patrick was at midnight. She wished she hadn't tried to call him at all, wished she could erase her fingerprints from the phone to erase the deed itself. What good was missing him when he obviously wasn't doing the same? She felt defeated.

"Katrina? Why don't you forget about Patrick and have some fun tonight?"

Chrissy must have read the slump in her shoulders. She took a deep breath and nodded. "That sounds like a great idea. Let's go."

Before they left the room, Katrina told Chrissy that she had to use the bathroom, that she'd meet her in a moment. Closing the bathroom door behind her, she sat on the closed toilet lid and cried softly, so no one could hear.

Chapter 7

Katrina wandered back into the party, realizing that she hadn't eaten anything all night. The crowd had thickened, and the lamps were turned down lower, the music louder. The number of smokers had multiplied, and the smell of burning tobacco overpowered the potpourri sitting on bookshelves and tables around the house. The heavy smoke stung her eyes, and she groped her way toward the kitchen, bumping into people she'd never seen before.

She stepped into the brightly-lit kitchen, stopping to let her eyes adjust to the brightness. She blinked and looked around the room. Linc was sitting at the round oak breakfast table, eating tortilla chips and guacamole with two other men. He smiled and waved her over. She might have made up an excuse to leave the room if her stomach hadn't been calling out for the chips and dip.

"Hey! I was looking all over for you. Where have you been?" Linc interrupted his conversation to rise and usher her to the remaining seat at the table, directly across from him.

She shrugged. "Oh, Chrissy and I were talking."

He introduced her to his companions as they stood to leave.

She nodded and smiled at them, thinking they looked vaguely familiar. "I think I went to high school with those guys," she said lightly, helping herself to some chips.

Linc pushed the dip closer to her. He watched with great

interest while she ate, but she was too hungry to feel self-conscious. When she slowed down, he brought her a glass of Coke.

"Thanks. Force of habit, huh?" she said, pointing to the glass.

"Maybe."

Katrina had expected him to laugh, but he stared at her solemnly. "I looked all over for you so we could finish our dance."

She felt it again, that spark of desire that she'd felt while they danced. It didn't creep up slowly like the last time. It was just there, without warning, a feeling that made her stay in the kitchen when she knew she should leave, find someone else to talk to, avoid Linc.

She'd never been comfortable in situations like these, trying to get to know someone before you were sure you really should. Dating had usually been precarious and tense for her. She always felt like she was missing something that other girls seemed to know about relationships that some had forgotten to tell her.

Her sophomore year in college, she'd gained twenty-five pounds, and the only guys who asked her out wore their pants two sizes too small and their hair two inches too long. Her junior year Katrina lost thirty pounds and dated guys who wouldn't pressure her to be their girlfriends.

Her senior year she swore off dating altogether. She went to aerobics class with Chrissy. She increased her letters to Patrick to twice a week. She had decided to enjoy her last year of college without the stress of dating.

But her mother had different ideas, especially after she'd moved back to Milwaukee after college.

"So, are you dating anyone?" Annie would ask hopefully.

"Mom, please, I'm focusing on my career right now."

"Can't you do both?" Annie's style was to badger until Katrina gave in.

"No." Katrina's style was to dig in and become even more stubborn.

"Katrina."

"Mother."

The silence was like a game of emotional chicken. Whoever spoke first lost the game.

"Mom, I have to go. It's late. I have to work tomorrow."

"My friend Lenore knows a nice young man, a lawyer."

"Mom, come on!" The types of men her mother chose for her were steady and staid, the kinds of men who would never surprise you.

"Just give it a chance, for me, please."

"Whatever, Mom. I've got to go. Good night."

Katrina was terrible at chicken and she went on countless dates with nameless lawyers, doctors, teachers, and accountants who bored her. Phil the lawyer loved to talk about the details of his cases, which might have been interesting if he'd been a trial lawyer. Since he did tax law, it was an effort not to yawn in his face. Benji the accountant worried her; what kind of a name was Benji for a grown man? For her mother's sake, she endured these dates. Plus, she held out a glimmer of hope that she might meet someone worthwhile among the geeks who were so desperate they had to be fixed up on dates. She didn't like to think that she apparently fit that category, too.

Sitting in Chrissy's kitchen, she had no idea what to say to Linc. She looked at him and tried to think of a clever comeback, to try to lighten the mood and silence whatever it was between them. She gave up.

"I don't think dancing is such a good idea." She remembered how her body felt pressed against his. Something inside her yelled "Run!" But another part of her, a voice that was quieter, more insistent, told her to stay, to find out more about Linc. Find out more about this ripple of emotion between them.

"Let's just hang out here for a while. I'm still hungry, and it's way too smoky out there," she added. "Plus, all I know about you is that you work at Vinyl, but there must be more to you than that."

He flashed his crooked smile at her, and it occurred to her how charming it really was. She listened while he talked about himself, waving for him to go on while she refilled their glasses.

She half-expected him to have some story about how he wasn't really a bartender by trade, that he was only doing this to work his way through school—the old bartender with a genius IQ who was going to be a millionaire someday. But he was finished with school, he said. He'd studied to be an accountant, but he quit after working at a small firm for a month. He chose bartending because it was easy and fun and he didn't have to think.

"After four years of college and one month of accounting, I needed to not think for a while," he said.

"How long have you been tending bar?"

"Since I was twenty-two. Four years."

"Are you still not thinking?"

"Now I'm thinking about what I really want to do with my life."

"What's that?"

"I haven't figured it out yet."

He loved playing softball, he said, pulling up his pant leg to show her where his knee was scarred from too many diving catches in the outfield. It never really healed, he said, so the skin was tender and fragile around his knee. He dreamed of living in London. He'd only been once, during a summer off from college, but he felt a sense of home there, like it was where he belonged.

"I wanted to spend my entire senior year studying abroad, but my parents couldn't afford it," he said, shrugging. "I knew they didn't have the money, but I applied anyway. It's dumb, but it just felt like if I could get accepted to the program, it was a sign that I belonged there, you know?"

Katrina nodded, wishing she knew what he meant, wishing she knew what it felt like to walk on foreign sidewalks and to feel like you belonged there. She tried to picture the cobblestone streets, the sound of the tube arriving into Victoria Station.

He hated dressing up. He said wearing a suit and tie felt like pretending to be someone else. He had even refused to be an usher at his sister's wedding because he couldn't bear the thought of a tux.

"But she's your sister."

"Please. We never got along. She doesn't even like me, and the only reason she invited me at all is because it would look bad not to have your own brother at the wedding. Plus, my parents insisted that she invite me. She didn't say a word to me the whole time," he scoffed.

"Why doesn't she like you?" Katrina was intrigued. She had no idea what it was like to have a sibling.

"Because I won't pretend to be what other people want. That's how *she* is, and she thinks everyone should be like her."

He never went to church, he said, not because he didn't believe in God but because he didn't believe you had to find Him in a certain type of building on a certain day at a certain hour. Katrina, who'd gone to Catholic school her whole life and grew up knowing the Mass by heart, wondered what it would be like to feel that free and confident.

"Do you ever think you might be wrong, that you might be missing something?" she asked carefully.

He considered that for a minute. "Sometimes I do wonder if I'm missing something. I'm just not sure I could find it in a church."

As he talked, her mind drifted. She noticed he hadn't mentioned a woman in his life, someone to convince him to wear a tie, someone who wanted him to go to church. If she asked, would it be obvious that she was interested? Katrina decided not to ask and was about to ply him with more questions about religion when she realized that the house was much quieter and she could no longer smell smoke coming from the other rooms. Jazz had replaced the dance music, and she didn't hear voices yelling and laughing outside the kitchen door. She couldn't remember when someone had last come into the kitchen looking for a bottle opener or another plate of cookies.

"Linc, what time is it?"

He glanced at his watch and started. "Umm, three-thirty."

She got up to peek out into the living room. A few couples still swayed to the slow, dark sounds of trumpets and drums or looked around for their coats. Katrina spotted Rick and turned back to Linc.

"Hey, I need to talk to Rick real quick. Be right back."

He nodded and started putting the dirty glasses and plates into the sink.

Katrina walker over to Rick.

"So, did you have fun?" he asked, holding a full ashtray in one hand and a broken goblet in the other.

"Yeah, I did, actually. Are you already cleaning up?"

He laughed. "Well, it's late, and almost everybody is gone, so it seemed like a good idea. Where have you been?"

She blushed. "In the kitchen talking to Linc."

"You guys must really be hitting it off," he said, smiling.

She nodded and felt guilty. She'd been so caught up with Linc that she hadn't thought about Chrissy, the party or Patrick for hours. "Hey, where's Chrissy?"

"Oh, she fell asleep awhile ago. She went into the bedroom to get something, and when I checked on her she had decided she needed a 'little rest.' Her last words were orders that I keep the party going," he smiled.

She didn't detect any hint of displeasure at being left alone. "That's really asking a lot. I would have forced her to stay awake," Katrina joked.

"But she was so tired. And she did so much work to put this party together, I figured it was the least I could do."

No wonder Chrissy loved this man, she thought. Who wouldn't? It suddenly occurred to her that she had no ride home. Chrissy had picked her up earlier in the day. "She didn't say anything about me getting home before she passed out, did she?"

"Nope. But I can take you home," Rick offered.

"Or I can," Linc said from behind her. She wasn't sure how she felt about his habit of sidling up without her noticing. He seemed to have some sixth sense that allowed him to show up at the perfect time.

She looked at Linc and knew it would be easier to let Rick take her home. She hadn't spent the last two hours getting to know Rick. She wasn't fascinated by Rick's family, his scarred knee. She trusted herself with Rick. But she knew he'd planned to stay over and help Chrissy clean up, and if he was staying she didn't want to hang around and get in their way.

It was probably a bad idea to be alone with Linc, in the car, at her apartment. Of course, if he asked to come in, she would say no. Wouldn't she? Definitely, she decided. She didn't need this kind of complication in her life. Hanging out at a party was one thing. Hanging out in her apartment was something else.

"Rick, I don't want you to go to the trouble. Linc's leaving anyway, so I'll get a ride with him."

"Are you sure?" Rick looked back and forth between Katrina and Linc.

She nodded and hugged him. "Thanks for the offer, though." She looked at Linc. "I'll get my purse and coat. Be right back."

Katrina watched her breath explode into white puffs then disappear into the cold air outside Chrissy's house. She pulled her leather jacket tight around her shoulders and turned the heat on high before settling down into the bucket passenger seat of Linc's car. The old tan Honda sedan hummed loudly when he started it, and with the heater forcing out gusts of cold air, Katrina felt blanketed by sound.

Linc reached over to turn the heat down, then handed her a thick, gray cable-knit cardigan from the backseat.

"It won't get warm for a while. Old car," he apologized. "Put on that sweater under your jacket, maybe you'll warm up."

They rode in silence, Katrina staring at a spot on the floorboard where the car had rusted through. There was no floormat, and she could see the black bumpiness of the street through the cherry-sized hole. White flashed when Linc turned a corner or changed lanes, then back to the dark pavement. When she squinted and held very still, the asphalt looked like lava running under the car. "Right here, left at the light, five miles down the road," was all she said, barely looking up as she directed.

She felt Linc looking over at her as she focused on the floor of the car, and she wished she lived closer to Chrissy instead of twenty minutes away. Those hours in the kitchen, when she was so relaxed, so comfortable, felt like another lifetime. Now she felt anxious and tense and wondered what he was thinking.

He didn't speak until they were three blocks from her apartment building. "So . . . I didn't get to hear much about you tonight," he said quietly.

"I figured Chrissy would have told you everything you needed to know," she said, pointing to her building. "This is me, stop here."

He pulled into a spot in front of her door and put the car in park. He turned toward her, leaned his head against the seat's headrest and looked at her. "You don't get to know someone through someone else."

She coughed uncomfortably and reached for her purse.

"Well, I better get inside." She grabbed the door handle.

He turned off the car. "I'll walk you to the door."

"No, you don't have to."

"Katrina, it's the middle of the night," he said, peering out the window into the still pre-dawn. "I'm walking you to the door."

They moved quickly, shivering in the late October air. Katrina fumbled for her keys and randomly thought that this would be the last time she could wear a short skirt before the snow came. She put the key in the lock and turned to Linc.

"Thanks for the ride. It was really nice of you," she said formally.

He smiled and waved a hand in the air. "Any time. I don't live far from here anyway." They stood at her front door, eyes locked, and it reminded Katrina of the day Patrick had returned. They'd stood in this same spot, taking each other in.

Then they'd made love for the first time on her living room floor.

Guilt bubbled up from her stomach. She hadn't thought about Patrick since she left Chrissy's bedroom. Maybe something legitimate had kept him from the party. She felt disloyal, confused. She broke away from Linc's gaze and opened the door. "I need to get in out of the cold," she said quickly. He nodded and leaned close, and she braced her lips for a kiss.

Instead, he kissed her on the forehead and squeezed her arm. "I had a great time tonight. But next time, we talk about you." He waved and walked back toward his car.

She stepped inside and closed the door, watching him through the side window. Next time? She blew into her hands before taking off her jacket. She walked through the apartment, turning on lights and turning up the heat, and she caught a glimpse of herself in the hall mirror. She was still wearing Linc's gray sweater. She pulled it off and folded it carefully. Next time.

Chapter 8

Monday morning after the party, Katrina got to work early after stopping for a bagel and apple juice on the way. She'd spent Sunday trying not to think, losing herself in *Bastard Out of Carolina*. The phone rang several times during the day but she didn't answer. Once, when she finally decided to shower around five o'clock, she thought she heard the doorbell. But she'd remained holed up, pretending that her life consisted of butter-flavored microwave popcorn, homemade chocolate-strawberry smoothies and a hapless girl named Bone whose bad luck seemed inevitable from the very first page. It wasn't exactly uplifting reading, but when she was feeling ungrounded, like a crinkled autumn leaf tumbling down an unfamiliar street, she liked to read about women whose mothers abandoned them, women who were doomed. It made her feel better about herself.

But now it was Monday and there was no pretending that she didn't have a pile of pink message slips on her desk. There was copy to write and concepts to pitch, another day to waste at a job that had recently turned from simply boring to nearly intolerable. A couple of weeks ago, in a moment of rare levity, she'd tried to convince her boss that no one would die if CP Foods didn't get their new ad campaign right away, that they should take more time and have some fun turning out a quality product. Elène, an embarrassingly thin woman with a beaked nose and an all-black wardrobe that reeked of cigarette smoke, whose real name, Katrina had discovered one day while searching for an old file, was Helen, had run her fingers through her sharply-sheared, dyed-black hair, pursed her plum-colored lips and told Katrina to get to work.

The absence of humor was just one of the things that Katrina hated about her job. The people she worked with reminded her of ants. At first she had admired the way everyone worked hard, the way they stuck together to get something accomplished. Then, after a while, she realized that what they were trying to accomplish was no good, it wasn't really going to help anyone and in fact, it was often insidious and poisonous. She'd tried to make friends at first, and for a while she felt like part of the colony. But they wore her out, with their singular focus and their endless happy hours and lunches at Chili's. Come celebrate Jen's promotion, the endless emails read. Join us as we congratulate Rob on getting a bigger office. Happy birthday to Lisa, Mel, Karen and Sue. Katrina wanted to feel interested in these celebrations, but she couldn't. Every time she went to one of the happy hours she thought she could hear the seconds of her life ticking slowly away.

After five years of working with these people, whose faces changed but dispositions did not, they'd come to a truce. They copied Katrina on the email invitations so as not to be rude, but they had a tacit understanding that she would not come. Katrina had finally realized that she preferred to be with Chrissy and the people she knew from the clinic. There was something about doing good for a living that made them much more palatable than people who created advertising to convince others to buy, buy, buy. Sometimes, Katrina hated herself—wasn't she doing the same thing, writing to fool people into believing that a certain furniture polish provided a better shine and a more lemony smell than the generic brand? But she reassured herself that at least she didn't believe what she was doing was right. She figured it must mean something when you *knew* what you were doing was wrong.

She got to work early that Monday after the party to get a head start on the piles of paper and the bleep of incoming emails. She sifted through the mess on her desk, making a to-do list and munching her bagel. The first call of the day came at 7:20.

"Katrina Larson."

"Hi, honey!" Her mother sounded cheerful and bright, trying too hard to be perky at this hour. Katrina was immediately on alert.

She set her bagel aside. "Hi, Mom."

"How are you?"

Now she was suspicious. Idle chitchat was not her mother's thing. Plus, shouldn't she be on her way to work? Wasn't Monday one of the days her mother worked as a nurse at St. Mary's School?

"Hey, are you at work already? I thought you didn't start until nine," Katrina asked, wondering what it would take to get her mother to say what she really wanted.

Annie cleared her throat. "No, I'm not going in today."

"Oh." They sat there in silence for a moment, each waiting for the other to carry the conversation. Katrina lasted only about 5 seconds.

"So what's up? How did you even know I was at work already?"

"I called you at home and you weren't there, so I figured I'd try you at work." Who calls her daughter at seven in the morning just to chat, she wondered.

"Did you want something?"

"Oh, I just wanted to talk," Annie said with false breeziness. "And I have a little bit of news."

Katrina perked up. "News? What news?"

"Well . . ."

"Mom."

"Well, I've met somebody," Annie blurted.

If Katrina didn't know better, she might have thought her mother actually giggled. Taken aback, Katrina stumbled over her words. "Met someone? Who? When? Why didn't you tell me?"

"Slow down! I'm telling you now. His name is Charles Mason. He's a college professor, widowed, and he's the smartest man I ever met," she said quickly.

Was there something in the air this fall? Everyone Katrina knew was falling in love.

"Wow. How long have you been seeing him? So when can I meet him?"

"Just a month or so. As far as meeting him, well, that's another reason I'm calling. He's got a conference in Milwaukee today, and I thought we'd take you out to dinner tonight. Are you free?"

Katrina quickly tried to calculate when she'd last talked to her mother. It hadn't been that long—why hadn't she brought up this Charles before? She'd have to wait and find out in person.

"Of course I'm free. See you tonight."

Katrina left work a few minutes early to shower and change before dinner. She felt a heaviness in her shoulders as she maneuvered through rush-hour traffic on Oakland, and the stress of the day clung to her skin like a fine layer of grit. The thought of going out to dinner was wearisome, even depressing, and she might have called her mother to cancel if she weren't so curious about this new boyfriend.

As traffic ground to a halt near North Avenue, she

searched the radio stations for music that would get her in the mood for dinner. Something upbeat. She settled on an old Duran Duran tune, "Rio," because at least it didn't make her feel like crying. She sang along with the chorus, thinking that these old lyrics lingering in her brain were the reason she couldn't remember where she put her keys or algebra.

As she pulled up to her street and parked, her singing faded. She noticed the car parked in front of hers. Patrick. By the time she got out of the car, he was standing near her door, a baseball cap pulled down over his eyes, wearing jeans and a gray Stanford sweatshirt.

After standing her up two days ago, he was here. Ready to explain and apologize? Ready to reveal his secrets? She got out of the car, grabbing her briefcase from the backseat. She didn't know what to say as they stood watching each other. The hurt she'd felt at the party had dissipated into a dull ache, and she just wanted to forget the whole thing. He wasn't wearing a coat, and she noticed him shivering slightly, his hands shoved deep into his pockets. He looked cold and vulnerable, and the sadness in his eyes made Katrina's chest tighten.

He cleared his throat. "I'm sorry. About Saturday."

She shrugged, unwilling to show him that it had mattered.

"Can we talk?" His voice was soft and low, and she heard a note of resignation behind his words.

She nodded. "Come in."

Patrick sat on the edge of the sofa, looking ill at ease. She tossed her coat onto a chair, telling him she'd be right back, that she needed to change. She didn't feel like she could face him before showering, like she needed a fresh perspective on whatever it was he had to say.

He nodded without meeting her eyes and picked up a *Glamour* magazine from the coffee table. As she walked down the hall to her bedroom, she heard the pages flipping in a steady rhythm that told her he wasn't bothering to read the words.

She showered in the hottest water she could stand, letting the steam loosen the knots in her shoulders. Drying off and applying her favorite peach-scented lotion, she quickly changed into a cream-colored wool sweater and wide black pants. She decided to leave off her heels until it was time to leave, and she pulled her wet hair back into a bun. She walked into the kitchen, where she could still hear the magazine pages flipping. He must have started over at the beginning, she thought. Either that, or he'd picked up a new one to not read.

"Coffee?" she called out to him.

"That would be nice." *Flip. Flip. Flip.*

She took her time making the coffee, searching the cupboards for the expensive Jamaican blend, rinsing out her favorite blue mugs, pouring cream and sugar into matching ceramic containers. She carried the whole production in on a tray, setting napkins and a small plate of chocolate chip cookies in front of Patrick, who put down his magazine and thanked her softly. She poured herself a cup from across the coffee table.

Now that there was nothing more to do, she moved her coat and sat in the chair facing the sofa, worried that whatever they would say would be tainted by close proximity.

He glanced at her, surprised. "You're pretty dressed up for someone who just got home from work."

She nodded. "I have to go out to dinner with my mom tonight. She's got a new boyfriend. Charles."

He raised his eyebrows. "Annie with a new boyfriend? Wow."

"My thoughts exactly, which is the only reason I didn't

call and cancel. I'm beat." She wondered if their conversation was going to go on like this, like nothing had happened, like everything was fine between them.

"I thought you looked a little . . . off. Tired or something. Well, how *are* you?" Patrick's voice sounded uncertain, as if he wasn't sure whether he wanted to keep pretending things were normal.

"Okay, I guess." Neither of them spoke for a while, the silence interrupted only by the occasional sound of their lips against the mugs. She didn't know what to do, what to say to make everything all right. She hoped he could say something that would.

He cleared his throat. "Katrina, I'm sorry."

This time, she knew he was talking about more than the party.

She started to speak, but he held up a hand to stop her. "I came here to tell you that you were wrong."

Katrina was incredulous, setting down her empty mug in frustration. "So this is the I'm-sorry-that-you-were-wrong apology? Great."

"Can you just be quiet for a second while I talk?"

She pursed her lips. "Go ahead."

"I *am* sorry, and you *were* wrong. You were wrong when you said that I don't care about your life and your friends. What's important to you is what's important to me."

"Then why couldn't you come to the party? Why was it such a difficult thing for you?"

Patrick put his head in his hands. "Katrina, I was scared. I am scared." His face was shielded by the cap he hadn't taken off.

"Scared? Of what?"

He looked up, and she saw the pain and frustration tighten the lines around his mouth. "Of this. Of you. Of us."

She sighed. "Who isn't scared? That's not an excuse, not after all we've shared. Not after we've known each other for more than half our lives."

He leaned forward on the sofa, the spoon he'd used for sugar clutched tightly in his hand. "I know. And I want to tell you all about the time I was away, about everything."

Everything? Katrina thought. Her stomach sank, and she remembered that old cliché about being careful what you wish for. She glanced at her watch in a panic. "I can't do this right now, Patrick. I have to meet my mother soon."

He looked flustered. "Now? We really need to talk about this."

She swallowed hard. "I really want to talk about it, too. But now? I just can't," she said quietly.

"How soon do you have to meet them? Maybe I could go with you," he said. "Then maybe we can talk afterward." It was almost as if he thought he would lose his nerve if he let her out of his sight. So eager to follow her, he looked younger, and with the baseball cap on he reminded her of the boy he'd been at age twelve, the one who'd stolen her heart with one childish kiss. She was scared to talk about "everything," scared of what he'd been keeping secret for months.

"You don't have to—"

"I know I don't have to. I want to." He looked into her eyes, imploring, and she couldn't say no.

She nodded. "Okay, but we're going to Cucina, and I think they have a policy against baseball caps."

He laughed. "Really? Those snobs. So I'll go home, change, and meet you there. What time?"

"Seven-thirty. Reservations under Larson."

She walked him to the door, and he paused and turned to her.

"I wish I had come to the party, you know. All I did all

night was sit home, ignoring the phone and wondering what you were doing," he said, taking off his baseball cap. His hair was mussed, and the wild curls sticking out all over his head made Katrina smile. She slid closer to him and leaned her forehead against his chin. He stroked her cheek as they stood there, barely touching, eyes closed. She felt his hand shaking a little, and she was sorry when he pulled away.

"I better go. See you in a while."

She nodded, and watched him as he fit his cap on his head before walking to his car.

Although she'd rushed Patrick out of her apartment, she didn't have much more to do except put on her shoes and drive to the restaurant, so she arrived early to Cucina. She handed her navy wool pea coat to the attendant and blew into her hands to warm them while she waited behind a Korean couple. When winter came to Milwaukee, it came quickly and stealthily, sneaking in through unbuttoned jackets and windows left unsecured. Her cheeks tingled from the sudden warmth of the restaurant, and she felt a slight ache in her ears from the icy wind she'd encountered in the parking lot. Katrina had never been to Cucina, only knew of its reputation, and she tended toward more casual dining. But her mother had insisted that it was Charles's favorite restaurant, so here she was.

Observing the couple in front of her, who held hands the entire time they were negotiating with the formal, mannered hostess, Katrina took in the large, dim dining room half-filled with handsome people sipping from heavy goblets. She checked her watch—only 6:55—and figured the room would be full by 7:30. She glanced down at her clothes and was thankful that she'd worn nice pants and a sweater instead of the nubby houndstooth blazer she favored on days when she was feeling down. She was nervous and edgy, not sure what to expect from her mother, from Charles, from Patrick. Her mother might say something embarrassing to Patrick, or Charles might ask the wrong question about their relationship. When she was nervous, punctuality became a compulsion, and so she was 35 minutes early.

"Will you be dining alone this evening, ma'am?" The silver-haired hostess revealed perfectly capped teeth as she raised her eyebrows at Katrina and smiled.

"I'm waiting for three other people—we have a reservation under Larson—but I think I'll wait at the bar until they arrive."

"Certainly. Right this way."

Katrina's heels sunk half an inch into the plush burgundy carpet surrounding the bar area. Several wooden bar stools were available and she claimed one, setting her square leather purse down on the bar.

"Cappuccino, please." The whirring sound of steaming milk, coupled with the hushed tones of people murmuring around her, was comforting. Her hands were still chilled and stiff, and she looked forward to the warm sweetness of the coffee. Her drink arrived in a delicate, bone-white cup and saucer, both rimmed with a vine of translucent blue roses. The set, along with the slim spoon that was surely real silver, reminded Katrina of weddings and hopes of happily ever after.

She picked up her cup carefully and leaned back against the stool, sipping and imagining what her mother's new boyfriend was like. She knew her mother hadn't smoked for years and she'd spent many meals listening to Annie complain that her food tasted of tobacco when she dined in the smoking section. But Katrina didn't know anything about Charles. Maybe he chain smoked, or enjoyed an after-dinner cigar.

She tried *not* to think about what Patrick would tell her later about his five-year absence.

She half-listened to two men in immaculate business suits and shiny shoes argue over whose family they would visit for the holidays. Katrina was rooting for the red-haired one—his voice was gentle and kind—when she spotted Annie at the door.

She tried not to show her surprise as she walked toward her mother. Annie, who had spent most of Katrina's childhood in jeans and long oxford shirts, wore a knee-length, formfitting dress of black jersey. Her mother had always tended toward plumpness, but now there was an unfamiliar sharpness to her shoulder blades, and her cheekbones were more pronounced. Annie's neckline dropped suspiciously low, and her long, dark hair was pulled up off her neck and held loosely with jeweled clips. Her lips were painted, her eyes lined in shadow, and she had artificially supplied the blush in her cheeks. It had been a long time since Katrina had seen her mother this dolled up.

"Have you been waiting long, honey?"

Annie pulled her close for a hug and she planted a kiss on her mother's cheek. Diamond studs adorned Annie's ears, and as far as Katrina knew, Annie hadn't owned any diamonds since she stopping wearing her wedding ring years ago.

"Hi, mom. I had coffee while I waited for you and Patrick."

Her mother raised her eyebrows. "Patrick's coming?"

Katrina nodded and turned to look at Charles, who stood quietly waiting during the embrace.

"Charles, this is my Katrina," Annie announced proudly.

Katrina tried to look calm and welcoming. He must have been 6'4", towering over both women, and she reached out to shake his hand. "It's nice to meet you," she said.

Charles turned to Annie. "Ann, she's even prettier than you described."

Smiling politely at his flattery, she finally got over her surprise at her mother and took him in.

Long and lean, Charles called to mind an ex-basketball player who'd given up the game before it ruined his knees and back. When he carefully handed Annie's coat to the attendant, he moved with the smooth coordination of a natural athlete. Perhaps he'd once run back and forth on parquet floors, but he now looked like a man concerned with more cerebral pursuits. His neat salt-and-pepper hair, woolen blazer and oval tortoiseshell glasses gave him a scholarly air. His unlined butterscotch skin and wide forehead made Katrina wonder if he was part Native American, like her mother. A beard that was still more black than gray surrounded his generous mouth, and he laughed easily at Annie's self-deprecating remarks about her tendency to brag about her daughter. Katrina watched the way he curled his arm around her mother's waist as the hostess with the perfect teeth led them to a non-smoking table.

They sat looking at menus and unfolding their crisp linen napkins when Patrick arrived.

"Sorry I'm late. Hi, Mrs. Larson. You look beautiful," he smiled at Annie, leaning over to kiss her cheek. "And you must be Charles? Nice to meet you." He shook hands with Charles and squeezed Katrina's shoulder before sitting next to her. "Hey, hon."

She raised her eyebrow at him, glancing pointedly at his blue wool blazer and neatly pressed khaki trousers. He was really going all out tonight, and somehow the effort made her feel more at ease.

Annie mock-scolded Patrick. "Well, hey stranger. I was

wondering when you were going to come see me."

Patrick shrugged sheepishly. "Mrs. Larson, you know I love to hang out with you, but Katrina has been taking up all my time."

Katrina laughed. "Oh, right, blame me."

Charles looked on with interest. "Patrick, how long have you known Katrina?"

"Oh, it seems like all our lives, but I guess since we were about twelve," he said.

Katrina shifted in her seat, sensing an uncomfortable line of questioning coming and wondering how Patrick would respond.

"So you've been an item all that time?" Charles asked.

Patrick shook his head. "I think there was always something there, even when we were kids, but we just recently realized there was more to it."

Katrina looked down at her menu, surprised that he would admit this in front of other people.

"Charles! Don't interrogate the boy before we've even ordered," Annie joked.

Charles chuckled. "Okay, okay, but over dessert I insist on hearing his entire life story."

This exchange between Charles and Patrick relaxed Katrina a bit. They made small talk about books they'd read recently, the sudden change in weather, her job. Charles was eager to engage her in conversation, and while they talked, Annie touched his hand when she asked him a question or prodded him to tell one anecdote or another. He called her mother "Ann" and gazed at her just a beat longer than necessary when she spoke.

"Have you decided what to order?" Annie asked. Katrina shook her head and glanced down at the menu.

"I'm not sure. Everything looks so good."

"Why don't you try the grilled salmon? It's been fantastic every time I've had it," her mother suggested. Every time? Her mother must have come over from Madison many times to eat here with Charles.

"I've had the grilled salmon. It's great," Patrick chimed in.

Katrina shot a glance at him. Since when did he go to Cucina? He winked, and she rolled her eyes. He'd never even been here before; he was just charming her mother. And successfully, at that, since Annie was nodding approvingly at him.

"Grilled salmon it is, then," Katrina said, sipping from her water glass to hide her amusement at Patrick's bullshitting.

They ordered, and after the waiter left, Annie said, "I'm pleasantly surprised to see you, Patrick. Katrina said she didn't think you'd be coming tonight."

Both her mother and Charles looked at Patrick expectantly, and she hoped he wouldn't bother to tell them about their earlier conversation.

"Oh, I thought I had plans, but they fell through," he said, glancing at Katrina. "And, it's been so long since I saw you, Mrs. Larson."

Annie looked between the two for a moment before she answered. "Patrick, you look great. Traveling seems to have treated you well. Where were you again?"

Patrick cleared his throat. "All over, really, but I spent lot of time in Asia and Europe."

"And Katrina said you were with college friends, right? Steve or James, or something?"

Katrina felt her cheeks warm with embarrassment. Her mother had no qualms about grilling anyone.

Patrick answered uneasily. "Yeah, Steve, Jamie, Marion. We all went to Stanford together."

"It's great to bond like that with your buddies," Annie said.

Patrick looked strained as he nodded.

Katrina shifted in her seat and turned to Charles. "So, Mom told me you had a conference to attend today. Work-related?"

With Annie beaming at his side, Charles explained that he taught history and literature to graduate students at Marquette. He enthusiastically described his presentation on the Harlem Renaissance, and Patrick asked detailed questions that clearly impressed Charles. Katrina's mind wandered. She considered whether it would be rude to ask more personal questions. Had he ever been married? Did he have kids? How had he and Annie met?

Annie interrupted Patrick's questions to describe how well received Charles's presentation had been, and Katrina noticed how comfortable they were together. Charles seemed to know just when to call for a refill on Annie's Chardonnay. Annie felt completely at home peppering his stories with her own editorial comments. They reminded Katrina of a married couple that has settled into a pleasant companionship, and she remembered what her mother had said on the phone that morning. They'd been dating a month or so, she'd said. But there was none of that uncertainty that crowds a young relationship. They had found a rhythm as a couple, and she guessed that they had been seeing each other quite a bit longer than a month. When she looked over to see Patrick's reaction, his curious expression showed that he also suspected something more than a casual relationship.

Katrina felt a little left out, as if Annie was keeping a part of herself deliberately hidden. She felt an odd sense of loneliness, and as she cut into her tender salmon, she tried not to resent the camaraderie between her mother and Charles.

Seeing the look on Annie's face, she knew she should be happy for them.

After they ate and ordered coffee, Patrick and Charles decided they needed cheesecake, and Katrina excused herself to the restroom. She splashed warm water on her cheeks and slowly brushed her hair. She was exhausted. It had been a long day, and it didn't show any signs of ending, with this impending talk with Patrick. She was peering at the tiny lines that had appeared around her eyes when Annie walked in. She put her arm around Katrina's shoulders, and they looked at each other in the mirror.

"Are you okay?" Concern dug ridges in Annie's forehead. Even so, it struck Katrina how vibrant her mother looked, how a sensual peace seemed to radiate from her pores.

Katrina didn't have the energy to lie. "Not really. I mean, I'm fine, I guess. Just tired."

Annie nodded. "It's good to see Patrick after all these years. What's going on with you two?" She had a way of cutting through her daughter's defenses, seeing what was really going on in her mind. It had vexed Katrina as an adolescent, this maternal mind reading, but this time she felt relieved not to have to pretend, if only for a few minutes in a plush ladies' room.

"He and I just need to talk, that's all, Mom," she said, looking down at the way she and her mother were reflected in the brass sink fixtures. Distorted, attached—Siamese twins connected at the shoulder.

Annie raised her eyebrows. "Fight?"

Katrina shrugged. "Kind of."

"Want to talk about it?"

Katrina put her hairbrush back in her purse. "Maybe some other time. Not now."

Annie squeezed Katrina's shoulders. "Okay." She cleared

her throat. "You know, Charles really likes you a lot. He likes Patrick, too." She removed her arm from Katrina's shoulder and turned to fix her own makeup.

"He really likes *you* a lot," Katrina teased. "And, by the way, you look gorgeous."

Annie glowed. "He went on and on about how smart you are."

"I like him, too. He really seems to care about you."

Annie turned to Katrina and nodded thoughtfully. "We really care about each other," she said.

Katrina wiped a smudge of excess powder from her mother's cheek. "Why didn't you tell me about him before? It's been longer than a month, right?"

Annie sighed. "Honey, I wasn't trying to keep secrets from you. I just wanted to be sure it was real before I told you, or anybody. I didn't want to jinx it."

"Is it real?"

"I think so. I really do," she said happily.

She smiled and hugged her mother, smothering any envy. She wished happiness hadn't been so elusive for Annie. They pulled apart, and Katrina noticed tears on her mother's face. She took out a handkerchief to blot her cheeks.

"Mom, why are you crying?"

Annie sniffed lightly. "It's just, you know, Charles is the first man that has meant anything to me, since . . ."

"Since Daddy." They looked at each other, and Katrina felt a flash of anger at her father. Maybe if he'd been around these last ten years, letting go would have been easier for Annie. Maybe it would have made things easier for both of them.

"Are you all right with this? I know how much you loved your father."

Katrina leaned over to peck her mother on the forehead. "I

think it's about time. You deserve to be happy. You deserve someone like Charles."

Annie reached out for her daughter's hand and held it. "So do you, Katrina. I hope you can find that with Patrick."

Katrina sighed. "Me, too." She held her mother's hand as they walked back into the dining room.

Chapter 9

Katrina and Patrick left the restaurant with their shoulders touching, calling promises of holiday plans back to Annie. Patrick walked Katrina to her car, the wind whipping his scarf around his neck, and as she reached for the door handle, he pulled her into his arms. They stood very still, her cheek pressed against his chest. Melded together, they were like a sculpture carved of soft wood. Yet, there was something just a little uncomfortable about the position of their arms, the set of their shoulders. Katrina closed her eyes and tightened her hold on him, listening to the faint gurgle of his stomach through his camel overcoat. She felt his hands smoothing back her hair, and she looked up at him.

"Patrick." She unlocked her arms from around his waist and tried to pull away, but he held on to her.

"Not yet."

"Not yet, what?"

"I don't want to let you go. Not yet," he said.

"I wanted to thank you for coming."

"Do you have to let go for that?"

She smiled and leaned close again.

He squeezed her. "Thanks for letting me come. I needed to be with you tonight," he said softly.

"It helped, having you there. It was less tense."

"Charles seems nice."

They stood entwined for a few more moments, until the coldness of his coat buttons against her cheek made Katrina realize that her feet were getting numb from the cold.

"It's freezing," she said.

He squeezed her tight once more and let her go. "I'm sorry."

She opened the car door and looked at him.

"Are you coming over? I mean, are we going to talk?"

He nodded slowly. "I'll meet you at your place in a while." He leaned over and kissed her on the cheek, near her earlobe. "See you soon."

She watched him jog back to his parents' car and followed him out of the parking lot. But instead of heading straight home, she found herself driving alongside the lake with the window cracked and the heater on full blast. The wet, metallic smell of winter combined with the warm, dry air felt good. She slowed down to the speed limit, and the weedy smell of Lake Michigan intensified. She wasn't ready to go home just yet, so she parked near the rocks where she'd spent countless adolescent nights whispering with Patrick.

Even on a Monday night in October there were a few cars parked at odd angles in the lot. Teenaged girls sneaking out with the wrong guy, she guessed. Maybe fathers trying to convince themselves not to run away. Middle-aged women listening to the lake freeze.

Buttoning her coat to the top, Katrina got out of the car and climbed onto the rocks piled several feet above the water, careful not to wedge her heels into the cracks but not caring whether seaweed and sand stained her pants. She stuffed her hands into her pockets and watched errant lights blink mysteriously over the calm, inky water. She thought about her mother and Charles, wondering briefly if they would spend this cold, clear night together. She thought about Chrissy, who'd called yesterday to apologize for falling asleep at the party. She'd let the machine pick up because she hadn't wanted to talk about Linc.

The slosh of the waves lulled her into a sluggish relaxation, and Katrina thought about Linc's gray sweater, wondering where he was at that moment. She remembered their dance and the way he shared himself so easily. She could still smell the light, detergent scent of his sweater, and a guilty tingle warmed her belly.

Car doors slammed and engines revved in the lot behind her, and she knew it was time to go home. She took one final look down the beach and thought about the last time she'd been here. With Patrick, only weeks ago. They'd been playful and content, kissing and laughing in the August sun. She had expected to feel relieved when she and Patrick finally talked about the five years he'd been glossing over. But the prospect of their talk, the "everything" he planned to share, made her nervous. She supposed she was relieved that he was going to reveal his secrets; she just wished he didn't have any secrets. Still avoiding this wasn't going to do any good. Her steps were purposeful as she walked to her car, the clack of her heels echoing through the near-empty lot.

For the second time that day Katrina pulled up to her apartment to find Patrick waiting for her. Sharing food and family had loosened some of the awkwardness between them, and he took her hand as they walked to the door.

This time he had not made the mistake of coming without a jacket, and she briefly teased him about the fact that his collar was raised to cover half his face.

"Nice look."

"Winter's no time to worry about looking good."

"Obviously."

He sniffed and waved her off. "Just open the door, smart-ass."

The jovial mood lasted only a moment. As soon as Katrina

closed the door behind her, she felt lightheaded with anxiety. She kicked off her heels and went to pour two glasses of wine. She had the feeling that this talk might require something stronger than coffee. They sat next to each other on the sofa, and she was glad Patrick couldn't look right into her eyes.

He took a sip of the red wine before clearing his throat. She covertly glanced over at the slight slump of his shoulders.

She spoke before he had a chance to begin. "I miss you. Not just the last few weeks, but ever since you came back. I miss the way we used to be. Remember? When we used to share everything?" She said the words quickly, as if to fast-forward past this discomfort.

He nodded. "I remember."

She saw uncertainty in the set of his jaw, in the way he swallowed too often. "Just say whatever it is you have to say." She dug her fingernails into the soft leather of the couch and stared at a hairline crack in the white wall behind him.

"It's not that easy."

"Just do it, okay?"

He blinked. "Remember I told you about the friends I traveled with?"

"Yeah, Steve, Marion, some guy named Jamie. So?"

Patrick looked down at his sneakers and sighed. It was one of those heavy sighs, carrying the weight of a thousand missed opportunities and broken promises.

"Well, Jamie . . . she's more than just a friend."

"She?" Katrina whispered this. Her thoughts jerked through her mind like the pictures in a Viewmaster toy. Jamie. Jamie was a woman. Jamie was more than a friend.

"Yeah. She. Like I said, she's not just a friend." He paused and fidgeted.

"What?" she croaked, closing her eyes.

"My fiancée."

The air was thick and mute, no clock ticking in the background, no rustling of pants legs, no hum of fluorescent lights. There was only Katrina's irrational certainty that if she didn't move, didn't unclench her fingers, didn't open her eyes, then this would all be like one of those falling dreams where you wake up just before your brain splatters on the mottled pavement.

The sound of Patrick's breathing broke the spell. When she tried to move her hands, she found that her fingers had fallen asleep. She couldn't look at him, so she slowly rubbed her palms together to restore circulation. She could feel him watching her, and he cleared his throat as if he were readying himself to say words that hadn't quite come to him yet. She hoped he wasn't going to say he was sorry or try to make her understand his point of view. She didn't think she *could* understand how he had lied to her, how he had let her believe she was the only one for him. He'd rushed back into her life and given her faith in destiny, and with a few words he'd stolen away her belief that some things, some people, are meant to be. This was not part of her dreams of living happily-ever-after—the prince was not supposed to be engaged to someone else.

She kept rubbing her hands together. Maybe if she rubbed forever he would keep quiet forever, and they'd be found there like mummies years later, his lips pursed in infinite silence, her hands gnarled and locked.

"Katrina," he said.

His voice was infuriatingly calm and reasonable, and she hated the sound of her name on his lips. "What?" she spat.

"Talk to me." She looked at him, incredulous. He winced. "Okay, would you at least listen to me talk?"

She shrugged, mentally groping for a reply that was at least ten times worse than "Fuck you."

She listened in disbelief while he explained that Jamie *was* just a friend at school. Then they'd decided, with a few other people, to travel, and their relationship had progressed. He described how, three years after college graduation, they'd "fallen in love, I guess," and a year ago they'd decided to get married.

She felt like gagging while he talked about how he'd started having doubts right after they set a date, and how he'd come home "to think about things" in August.

Nonsensically, she asked, "What's the date?"

"What?"

"The date. Your wedding date." Somehow it was important that she know. For some reason it mattered.

"New Year's Eve."

She sighed.

He cleared his throat again. "Katrina. I still love you."

His voice was quiet and sad. She wondered if he felt bad because he'd lied or because she hadn't simply fallen into his arms and forgiven him. She noticed that he hadn't said anything about breaking the engagement or canceling the wedding. It was as if he thought his "I love you" was enough to gloss over the details of his lies.

She felt tears collecting in the back of her throat, in the corners of her eyes. Ridiculous, really, that he had the nerve to say this to her now. She turned to him without caring that her eyes had begun to drip and her voice shook. "Get out. Just get out."

Patrick stared at her, then rose and left. She waited until the door clicked shut behind him before burying her head in her hands.

After a long while, she got up, leaving the lights on and the full wineglasses untouched. She lay on the bed, staring at the ceiling. A host of thoughts rattled around in her head. Would this tightness in her throat ever go away? What would she tell her mother and Chrissy? Where was Jamie? Was she pretty?

But she didn't cry. Tears were not enough. She could cry for days and never shake this loneliness. She could cry for days and it wouldn't make a bit of difference. He had lied to her for months, years, really, with his silence about Jamie, someone who was obviously an important part of his life. Engagements could be broken, but she didn't know how to restore her trust in him, and no amount of tears could change that. So she just lay there.

The next morning, before her alarm clock buzzed, before darkness released its hold on the day, Katrina called in sick. If she'd slept that night, it had only been for a few minutes at a time. She was nudged awake by a series of disturbances: a car door slamming somewhere on her street, a distant siren, the sound of her refrigerator humming intermittently. Background noises preoccupied her all night, and by five o'clock she felt almost sick.

She padded into the kitchen, shivering in the draft, and left a voice mail for her boss. She crawled back into bed, dragging the cordless phone with her and rubbing her goosebumped arms. Back in bed, she cocooned the comforter around her. A deep chill hugged the apartment, and Katrina wished she could spend every winter morning snuggled in her bed, protected from obligations. The blankets were still warm from her body heat, and she finally dozed off as the pale sun began to peek through her curtains.

She dreamed of laughing girls, twelve years old and giggling about boys and hair and school. She dreamed of her mother as she was years ago, plump and young, promising to make waffles if Katrina agreed to drink a glass of whole milk. She was dreaming of eating a feast of fried chicken and brownies, cheesecake and pizza, when the insistent ring of the phone jolted her awake. She listened groggily, the taste of garlic and mushrooms still in her memory, as the answering machine picked up.

"Hi, you've reached 555-8162. I can't take your call right now, but please leave a message and I'll get back to you as soon as possible." Every time she listened to her own message she thought about how it sounded nothing like her.

"Katrina? I've been calling you since Sunday—call me back. This is Chrissy." She recognized the irritation underneath her best friend's carefully cheerful tone. She curled up tighter and tried to recapture the bliss of eating without concern for nutrition or cellulite. But a few minutes later the phone rang again.

"Are you there? I called you at work and they said you're sick. Are you okay? I should have called work first. I wouldn't have been so snotty if I knew you were sick. Bye. Call me. Bye."

Chrissy often left long, nonsensical messages. She got on a roll, wrapped up in what she wanted to say and the frustration of not being heard. Katrina closed her eyes. She wasn't sure how long it was until the next time Chrissy called, but she couldn't get back to sleep. She wished she'd unplugged the phone as she listened to Chrissy's voice for the third time that morning.

"K, I'm getting worried now. Do you need some medicine or something? Are you mad at me? This isn't about Linc, is it?"

Katrina, resigned, slithered one arm out of the covers to grab the phone. "Hello?"

"Oh, thank God! I was ready to panic," Chrissy said.

Katrina managed a dry chuckle. "You are so melodramatic."

"It's called concern, not melodrama. So what's wrong with you?"

She yawned deeply. "I'm just . . ." she stopped. How could she explain these confused feelings?

"Hello? You're just what? You were fine the last time I saw you." Chrissy sounded impatient and worried.

"Yeah, just before you passed out at the party and left me with Linc," she scolded.

"I *fell asleep,*" Chrissy retorted with mock haughtiness. "But speaking of Linc—"

Katrina frowned into the phone. "Don't want to talk about it," she snapped.

Chrissy sucked her teeth. "Fine. Nice attitude."

"Sorry."

"You never answered me. What's wrong with you? Are you really sick, or is it something else?"

"Something else."

There was an expectant pause. Chrissy sighed. "You know what, either tell me or don't. I have to get back to work."

Katrina immediately regretted the conversation, but she didn't have the energy to lie. Why should she? "It's Patrick."

"Now what?"

"Can you come over after work? It's a long story."

"He's not leaving again, is he?"

Katrina started. She hadn't thought that far ahead yet. About what she was going to do. About what he was going to do. About where to go from here.

"I don't know. Just come over."

"You'll be okay until then?"

She nodded even though Chrissy couldn't see her. "See you after work."

Katrina didn't leave the house that day. The phone rang a few times, but she didn't answer, letting the machine pick up.

But whoever it was didn't leave a message, and she was glad not to hear taped voices wondering if she was home, wanting her to pick up the phone, asking that she call them back.

She felt as if she was inside one of her recurring dreams, the one where she kept trying to catch the right bus home, but every route was going farther and farther away from where she needed to be. Endless transfers, repeated attempts to turn back toward the right direction, all yielding nothing but more distance. This was how Katrina felt each time she tried to think of something other than Patrick, something other than the seemingly infinite number of questions that kept popping into her head. Did his parents know? Would he have told before the big day if she hadn't forced the issue? Was he really in love with Jamie? How would he explain the last few months to his fiancée? Did Jamie know about Katrina?

Distraction was what she needed. Something mundane. She thought about going to the bookstore to pick out a new book, or heading over to The Ground Floor for a fresh supply of mocha-flavored coffee. But the temperature, according to Channel 3 meteorologist John Coblan, was twenty-five degrees, and the last thing she wanted to do was dig out her heavy parka and boots. So she stayed in her favorite terry robe all day, watching premature news features on Thanksgiving (only 32 days until Turkey Day!) and inane talk shows.

By the time Chrissy rang the doorbell, she'd seen housewife makeovers, laughed at a thwarted a fight between triplets separated at birth and shuddered at the senseless murders of three high school cheerleaders. The turmoil and tragedies of others helped dull her senses, and she buried herself in an orgy of trashy television punctuated by "Golden Girls" reruns.

When Chrissy arrived, Katrina turned down the volume and padded over to the door.

"Wow—what's all this?" Katrina grabbed three paper bags from Chrissy's arms.

"Dinner." Chrissy smiled and jogged back to her car for more bags.

Katrina started taking out the food. "Dinner for how many?" She eyed three bottles of wine, two heads of lettuce and several packages of fresh pasta.

Chrissy set down the last of her bags and shrugged. "I figured we'd be here a while. You said it was a long story, right?" She turned and eyed Katrina critically. "Have you been sitting around here in *that* all day?"

Katrina pulled her worn pink robe around her and tightened the belt. "It's cold. Might even snow," she said defensively.

Chrissy snickered and shook her head. "You need a new robe."

Katrina raised her arms to look at the robe. "Why? I've had this since college."

"No kidding. At least I know what to get you for Christmas."

Katrina smiled. "A car with seat warmers, a house with an attached garage and a handsome chauffeur?"

Chrissy laughed. "And a new robe."

They ate gourmet spinach rolls and wine, rinsing out the glasses Katrina and Patrick had left untouched the night before. It reminded Katrina of the things she'd been deliberately *not* thinking about all day, and she released a heavy sigh. They sat at the dining room table and Chrissy put the plate of rolls within their reach near the corner of the distressed oak table.

"So tell," Chrissy said, folding one of her legs underneath her. She grabbed a roll and waited.

Katrina began by telling Chrissy about Monday morning,

how she'd been dragging until she got the call from her mother.

"A new man, right? Annie's in love?" Chrissy interjected, leaning forward.

"Can you let me tell the story?"

"Can I get an abridged version?"

"No!"

Chrissy rolled her eyes. "Go ahead."

Katrina fast-forwarded to after work, when Patrick reappeared at her doorstep after three weeks.

"He had the nerve to just show up?"

Katrina nodded. "He was waiting for me when I got home."

Chrissy tsked. "He could have at least called."

"I wasn't taking his calls."

"So? He never heard of an answering machine?"

Katrina shrugged. "Anyway . . ." She talked about dinner, how incredible Annie looked, how perfect Charles seemed, how Patrick was on his best behavior.

"Of course he was! He was trying to get back into your good graces."

"And you want to know why?" Katrina felt her own anger rising in conjunction with Chrissy's.

"I'm afraid to ask."

"He's engaged." Just saying the words out loud made it seem more real. It was easier to pretend nothing had happened, that she really was just sick today. It was easier to tell Chrissy the story as if it were about someone else's life, not her own. But saying it out loud—"He's engaged"—was agonizing.

They sat silently looking at each other. Katrina wished that Chrissy would know what to say to make her feel better, but Chrissy's gaping mouth made words of comforting wisdom seem unlikely. Katrina watched the various reactions flash across her friend's face. Disbelief. Pity. Frustration. Sadness. Anger.

"That asshole," Chrissy said softly, her voice trembling.

Katrina's mouth felt dry, so she gulped down her Chardonnay.

Chrissy held her palms up and out, incredulous. "Engaged? Who? Since when? How could he not mention something like that?" She cut herself off and shook her head.

She answered Chrissy's questions in a monotone. Some girl he traveled with. Jamie. Since a year ago. Each answer drove home the truth: Patrick had been lying to her since he returned.

"Jamie is a girl? And what's he doing back here, then?"

Katrina scowled. "He said he came home to think about things. And get this—he had the audacity to tell me he still loves me." Katrina felt her face heat at the memory.

Chrissy scoffed. "He is so, so—I can't even think of a word." She took a long drink of wine and looked at Katrina. "So, how are *you?*"

Katrina thought about it. She felt hurt, of course. Confused. Shocked. But most of all, she realized, she felt like an idiot. "I just wish I hadn't let him do this to me. I shouldn't have been so . . ."

"Trusting," Chrissy finished for her. The unspoken "I told you so" hung low between them, clouding their thoughts and thickening their tongues.

Katrina looked away, embarrassed at her weakness. She should have known it would be something like this. She should have known, after fifteen years of friendship, that the thing he couldn't tell her would be something this important.

"So what are you going to do? How did you leave it?"

"I don't know."

"Well, what are you going to say to him?"

"Say? I don't want to talk to him." Katrina decided as she spoke.

Chrissy looked doubtful.

"Forget it, Chris. Let him go back to Jamie. Or not. Whatever. I'm not talking to him." She folded her arms.

Chrissy held up a hand. "I'm not saying you should kiss and make up. But he's been your best friend for so long."

"That didn't seem to matter to him." Her voice rose angrily, and as she watched Chrissy's eyebrows arch, she tried to calm down. "Right now, I just don't have anything to say to him."

Chrissy nodded slightly. "Look, let's cook dinner, open another bottle of wine and get sloppy, ridiculously drunk. Then maybe I can pry you out of that ugly robe, and we'll go out and have some real fun."

Katrina nodded and followed Chrissy into the kitchen.

Chapter 10

Homemade pasta and salad made with field greens, garlic bread, peanut butter cookies, rich vanilla ice cream and another bottle of wine allowed Katrina a temporary amnesia, the kind that let her put Patrick and Jamie out of her mind. She laughed loudly at Chrissy's wild stories about her co-workers, happy to hear about the problems of others for a change. She tossed back her hair, and looked critically down at the robe that now hung open, revealing the wrinkled T-shirt and boxer shorts she'd worn all day.

"Hey, let's go out."

Chrissy peered at her incredulously, pouring herself another glass of wine. "Go out? It's eleven o'clock on a Tuesday. Go out where?"

Katrina shrugged. "You mean to tell me *you're* not up for it? College kids go out every night, remember? Vinyl must be open."

"You hated Vinyl," Chrissy noted.

Katrina waved a hand at her. "Maybe I changed my mind," she said cheerfully.

Chrissy burped delicately. "Maybe you've had too much to drink."

Katrina laughed. "I thought you were the one desperate to get me out of this robe and out on the town. Come on, don't be such an old woman! Let's get dressed and go."

Chrissy thought a minute. "Okay. But you have to let me borrow a top to wear."

Katrina jumped up. "I'll find you something cute, and you call a cab."

Dressed in black, Katrina and Chrissy piled their hair on top of their heads, slathered on too much makeup and smuggled their glasses into the taxi.

"I feel like I'm in college again," Katrina whispered in the backseat.

Chrissy snickered. "High school," she corrected.

They surreptitiously slurped from their glasses, ignoring the disapproving look of the driver, who clearly didn't want to spend the rest of the night wiping wine off his imitation leather seats.

Inside Vinyl, Katrina briefly reconsidered the wisdom of going out on a Tuesday night. The club was filled with college kids clad in jeans and sweaters. The club had transformed its dark, trendy glamour into dorm room chic, with pennants and framed articles about local colleges on the wall, 2-for-1 beer signs placed prominently and kegs set on platforms in two corners of the room.

"God, you don't think they're actually serving people from those?"

They watched as a young man with a scruffy beard, baggy green pants and a ponytail staggered over to one of the kegs to fill his dented plastic cup.

"They really go all out for college night," Katrina observed.

"We may be overdressed," Chrissy said wryly, shucking her heavy coat and handing it to an attendant.

Katrina raised her eyebrows and nodded. "Good. Let's dance."

They made their way out onto the dance floor and lost themselves in the thump and screech of the music. They danced until their hair stuck to their damp temples, until their feet throbbed in their fashionable, non-functional heels.

"Want a drink?" Katrina asked during a brief break in the music.

Chrissy shook her head. "I'm still woozy from all that wine, and I want to at least *try* not to be hung over tomorrow—" she glanced at her watch— "today at work."

Katrina shrugged. "I'm not feeling nearly as woozy as I'd like, so I'm going to get a drink."

Chrissy waved to her as a guy in khaki shorts, a sweater and a knit cap grabbed her hand and pulled her back into the bouncing, swaying crowd. Katrina wondered at the folly of wearing shorts during a Wisconsin winter and walked to the bar. She was standing next to a barstool, digging for money in her purse, and when she looked up, Linc was standing in front of her, a bar towel in one hand and a fistful of ones clutched in the other.

"Katrina?" He looked surprised, and his crooked smile caught her off guard. She saw a slight shadow around his mouth that hadn't been there a few days ago, and she wondered if he was growing a beard.

Katrina shoved the lipstick cases, post-it notes and crumpled coupons back into her purse. "Linc."

She hadn't had a chance to think of what she would say to him, and now he was right here, looking at her. She should say something clever and smart, nothing too inviting or obvious. Something that would make him laugh.

"Hi," was all she came up with.

He smiled uncomfortably. Maybe he was caught off guard, too. "Hi," he replied.

They stood there looking at each other for a long moment until they were interrupted by a woman waving a five-dollar bill and calling, "Bartender!" from the other end of the bar.

"I'll be right back."

Relieved, Katrina sat on a stool and finally retrieved her wallet from the bottom of her bag. While Linc was mixing the woman's brown, milky drink, she quickly repinned her hair. She had just enough time to swipe her lips with lipstick before he returned.

"So what are you doing here?"

She laughed, calmer now that she'd had a few minutes to gather herself. "Not happy to see me, huh?"

He shook his head and smiled. "I'm completely happy to see you. I just didn't expect to see you tonight."

"I didn't come here to see *you* tonight, if that's what you mean," she teased. He shrugged and relaxed.

"Who said you did? Although now I have to wonder."

"Oh please, you're not that fascinating." She rolled her eyes.

"I'm not?" He feigned incredulity.

"Definitely not. But since you're just standing there, can you get me a Sprite?" Suddenly she didn't want any more alcohol.

Linc soon set a tall glass on a coaster in front of her. He leaned forward, his hands stretched out in front of him against the bar.

"So why *are* you here? Where's your boyfriend?" he asked, craning his neck to look around the room.

She cleared her throat. "I'm here with Chrissy."

He nodded, waving at Chrissy's undulating figure on the dance floor. "I see her. She's with some idiot in shorts."

"When you drink a certain amount of cheap beer, temperature-appropriate dressing loses its urgency."

He chuckled, directing his gaze back at Katrina. "I've never had enough beer to get me to wear shorts after September." He turned to pour himself a glass of water.

"So where's your boyfriend?" he repeated, sipping.

Katrina shrugged. "I told you, it's just me and Chrissy tonight."

"That's not what I asked." He looked at her, and she busied herself with rearranging the straw in her soda and taking a long drink. She hoped that by the time she looked up, he would be ready to drop it. She saw by the inquisitive look in his eyes that he wasn't.

"He's not around," she evaded. Linc waited. She didn't want to talk about Patrick, but she didn't want to pretend that everything was fine between them. Pretending seemed too protective of Patrick.

"We broke up," she added, watching his reaction. She was ready to walk away if he smiled or joked or made a suggestive comment.

He frowned. "What happened?" He saw the closed look on her face. "I'm not trying to be nosy. It's just a little, well, a lot out of the blue."

She was surprised and touched that he was standing there looking at her like she was a fragile glass figurine in danger of breaking.

"I'm okay," she said quietly.

He tilted his head to one side. "Are you sure? Because you don't seem like the type to come to Vinyl on College Tuesday."

She smiled. "Maybe I like cheap beer and guys in shorts."

"Who doesn't? Refill?" he asked, pointing to her glass.

She glanced over at Chrissy, who was still dancing, this time with a better-dressed partner. She tossed her head back, as if to toss away thoughts of Patrick. "Sure. I'd love another."

She sat for a long while, watching Linc work and making small talk. Between customers, he asked her questions that made her laugh. She thought and prepared her answers carefully while he poured vodka and squeezed lemons.

"Wham," she said when he returned from making a sloe gin fizz for the guy in shorts.

"*Wham?* That's your favorite eighties duo?"

"Wham is a perfectly legitimate choice. What's yours?"

"The Eurythmics, of course."

"Ugh," she grimaced.

"What's wrong with the Eurythmics?"

"You mean besides the fact that they suck?" They laughed.

She glanced over at Mr. Shorts in Winter, who was daintily sipping his drink near the bar. "What kind of college kid drinks a sloe gin fizz?"

He shrugged. "Maybe he's a man of refined tastes."

"Oh, he's clearly that."

Chrissy walked up to the bar, fanning herself. "Hey Linc. I didn't think you'd be working tonight." She reached over to touch his arm affectionately and looked over at Katrina. "I thought you were coming back out to dance. You left me out there with those goofy guys."

Katrina laughed. "You seemed all right to me."

Chrissy rolled her eyes. "Please, you weren't even thinking about me. You were over here hanging out with the bartender getting free drinks." She winked at Linc.

"I *paid* for my drinks, thank you. And you won't believe who his favorite eighties duo is," Katrina retorted.

"Umm . . . The Thompson Twins?" Chrissy guessed.

Katrina and Linc laughed until their eyes watered.

"What?" Chrissy was indignant.

Linc wiped his eyes. "The Thompson Twins were a *trio,*" he said solemnly.

Katrina kept laughing.

"So what? The eighties were ages ago. I can't even remember what I did yesterday," Chrissy sniffed.

Katrina finally controlled herself. "Linc, you'll have to excuse her. She was a big Bon Jovi fan."

"Ouch." He winced.

Chrissy protested. "I was not. Okay, I was, but it was only for a brief time because Jeff Carmello liked them and we were dating at the time."

Katrina waved her off. "You don't have to explain yourself to me."

"Me neither," he interjected. "I can respect a woman who will listen to Bon Jovi in the name of love."

Chrissy nodded smugly. "At least *someone* understands me." She asked for a Coke and turned to Katrina. "So, you ready to go soon?" Chrissy said in a low voice. She glanced at Linc's back, her eyes narrowed just a bit.

"No. I thought you were dancing," Katrina whispered, frowning.

Chrissy looked weary. "I *was* dancing, but I'm tired. It's late. I have to work tomorrow."

"So go," Katrina hissed.

Chrissy was surprised. "At least walk me to the door," she insisted. Linc returned with her soda, which she gulped down quickly. "Okay, kids, it's getting late and we have to work in the morning. Hey, Linc, it was good to see you again. Maybe we'll have another party soon," she said cheerfully.

"Sure. Katrina, you leaving, too?" Disappointment flitted across his face.

"Yeah, she—" Chrissy tried to answer for her.

But Katrina overrode her. "No, I'm just going to walk her out."

After calling a cab on the pay phone near the cloak room, Chrissy grabbed Katrina's arm. "What are you doing?"

"Why are you grabbing my arm? And you should get a cell

phone. They're really cheap now."

"Katrina, what are you doing with Linc?"

"I'm not ready to leave." She took out her compact and checked her face in the small, oval mirror.

"How are you going to get home?"

"I'll take a cab." She smoothed her eyebrows and closed the compact.

Chrissy watched Katrina closely. "Alone?"

"Why? I thought you were the one who *wanted* me to hang out with Linc." Katrina folded her arms.

"I did. I do. But not like this," Chrissy retorted, handing her ticket to the attendant.

"Like what?"

"You're upset about Patrick."

"I'm fine. Don't I seem fine?"

Chrissy pulled on her coat. "No. You don't."

She sighed. "Stop worrying about me. Linc's a nice guy. He'll make sure I get home okay."

Chrissy shook her head. "I'm not worried about you getting home."

A car horn beeped outside. "There's your cab. I'll call you tomorrow," Katrina promised, ushering Chrissy out the door.

"Katrina," Chrissy called back to her.

But she had already turned away to go back into the club. She was relieved when she heard the door slam and the taxi roll away.

Back in the main part of the club, College Tuesday was stumbling to a close. Girls who had come there in packs were leaving with guys they knew slightly, heading toward unfamiliar dorm rooms and familiar disappointments. The unpaired girls looked lonely but relieved. Another night without a regrettable sexual entanglement wasn't necessarily a bad thing. The single guys laughed loudly and called each other by nonsensical nicknames, saving their best lines for luckier nights. They all donned layers of outerwear and began the parade out to waiting cabs, or, for the less fiscally solvent, slowly rolling buses that trolled the downtown area until the wee hours.

Katrina walked through the exiting crowd to the bar, where Linc was cleaning up.

"Almost closing time, huh?" She slid onto an empty stool.

He nodded. "You can hang around, though. If you want." He rearranged bottles on the counter and looked at her as if he thought she might run away at any second.

She felt unsteady, like the floor was wobbly and warped underneath her stool. "Maybe I should go call a taxi."

"I can take you home," he said, tentative.

"Nah, I can't ask you to do that *again,*" she said. "You must feel like my private chauffeur or something."

He smiled slightly. "Not at all." He paused. "But if you don't feel comfortable, I can call you a cab."

"Why wouldn't I feel comfortable?"

"I don't want you to think anything." His voice trailed off, and he wiped at a non-existent spot on the shining bar. She watched him rub until the repetition began to unnerve her.

"Think what?" She lightly placed her hand over his to stop the rubbing.

He looked down at their hands, her caramel-colored fingers touching his darker ones, as he spoke. "I don't want you to think that I'm trying to be slick, take advantage of you because you just broke up with your boyfriend."

Katrina wasn't sure if she suspected him of doing just that. She wasn't sure she even cared. She heard Chrissy's unspoken admonishments to be careful, to avoid jumping into something with Linc. She heard Patrick's crying, and his "I love you" rang in her ears. She wanted to drown them out.

"I don't think you would do that," she said, realizing it was true. For whatever reason, she didn't think Linc wanted to use her. "Plus, I'm the one who stayed, remember?"

He sighed, relieved. "Give me a few minutes to finish up, and I'll give you a ride."

They smiled cautiously at each other. She glanced down at their hands, still touching on the bar. Katrina tried to read his eyes but couldn't, and she pulled away for fear that he could read hers. "I'll go get my coat."

He remembered the way to her apartment. She smiled to herself when he made left turns in all the right places, even remembering to avoid the long light that never seemed to turn green. Had he been planning to pay her a visit, memorizing the route so he didn't have to wait for an invitation?

This time, when they rolled to a stop in front of her apartment, she wasn't worried about whether he would ask to come in. She was sure he wouldn't.

"It was nice to see you again so soon," he said. They walked slowly up the path to her door, even though the wind had picked up considerably since Katrina and Chrissy had gone out.

"It was a surprise," she agreed.

"A good one." They stopped at her door, and he turned to look into her eyes. "Tell the truth: Did you know I would be there?"

She looked down the street, listening to the sound of the wind blowing through the buildings, watching a small, fuschia glove snag on a bush, wondering who would be dragging their child to Boston Store the next day for a new pair of mittens.

"I didn't *know* you would be there. Tuesday night is sort of random." That was true, she decided. She hadn't believed he would be there. But maybe, somewhere down deep, she had hoped.

"Ah, but if you were more familiar with the club scene, maybe you would have known that Tuesday is College Night," he said softly.

"Maybe." She met his gaze and worked up her courage. "Are you tired?"

She could see the weight of the night on his shoulders, eight hours of serving drinks and smiles and banter. His eyes were rimmed with dark circles, and she'd caught him yawning during the drive home.

"No. Well, yeah. A little," he said. His gaze, however weary his body, was sharp. It never wavered from hers.

She cleared her throat and looked toward her neighbor's apartment. She could see Mrs. Collins's television flashing in the darkness behind the blinds.

"Too tired to come in?" She still looked away, thinking that no matter what his answer, Mrs. Collins's television would soon show just a steady frame of static. It was late. His silence dragged her eyes back to his. He looked thoughtful.

"Do you think it's a good idea?"

She shrugged. "I don't know."

"Katrina." He touched her cheek softly. His hands were cold. "I don't want to be the way you get back at Patrick. Is that what this is?"

She looked down at her feet. "I don't know the answer to that one, either." She looked up at him again. "I just know that I want you to come in."

Linc closed his eyes and sighed. His fingers slid from her cheek to touch a lock of hair that had fallen from her upsweep. He leaned closer to her and kissed her just in front of her ear where the errant piece of hair curled. She turned her head so that her lips pressed against his. His hands reached around her waist, touching the small of her back almost reluctantly.

She pulled away, grabbed his hand and tugged. He resisted for a moment, looking at her. She knew he was torn between that kiss and doing what was right. But she wasn't interested in right and wrong.

"Please?" she whispered, pulling him closer to the open door.

He nodded and followed her.

As soon as the door shut behind him, Katrina turned and began kissing him, hard. He murmured something, but she shushed him and pulled at his jacket, helping him slide it off his shoulders. She led him into the bedroom, afraid that if they stayed in the living room it would be too much like her first time with Patrick. Too many memories might make her doubt herself. She continued to kiss him while she tugged off his sweater and T-shirt, pushing him down on the bed. He looked dazed, his eyes half-closed, and she stepped back so he could watch her slowly kick off her heels and peel her tight black dress down over her shoulders, her hips, her thighs, until it lay crumpled next to her shoes and stockings. She watched his eyes follow her hands to her bra as she removed it, then her panties. She walked slowly toward him, his strong hands grabbing her hips and pulling her down on the bed with him. They tangled together, and Katrina thought about how different it was to be with someone new. She felt detached, as if she were watching their bodies move together from afar. She saw the way her legs wrapped around his, the way she bit his ear, and she wondered if it would make what Patrick had done hurt a little less.

Afterward, Katrina was still, trying not to think, listening to Linc's regular breathing. She thought he was asleep, so she turned to look at him. But he was lying on his back, staring at the ceiling.

"What?" she asked, pulling the blanket up to cover them both.

He closed his eyes for long moment. "This wasn't right."

She propped herself up on one arm. "What do you mean? It felt right, didn't it?" Her tone was light. She didn't want to get into a heavy discussion about the essential "rightness" of having sex with Linc.

He shook his head. "Don't do that. Don't make it into a joke, or make it seem like it doesn't mean anything."

She sighed. "Fine, what do you think it meant?"

He turned his head to look at her. "What about Patrick?"

"What about him?" She frowned. "Why would you want to talk about another man after what just happened?"

"Katrina. Remember the other night, I told you all that stuff about me, about my family?"

"So?"

"So it's your turn to let me in." He sat up, frowning. "Having sex is not how you get to know someone."

She sat up, too, and pulled the covers up to her neck. "Why are you pushing me to talk about Patrick? Why do you even care?"

"I don't want to be some one-night stand you used to forget about your boyfriend. I don't want to be just a story you tell your friends," he said seriously. She looked away. "If that's really all this is, then just tell me, and I'll go."

She took deep breaths to keep from crying but it didn't work; the tears ran down her face. Linc pulled her to him and gently wiped the tears away with his fingertips. She couldn't talk, so she leaned into his chest and sobbed.

"Just tell me what happened with you and Patrick," he said when she'd quieted.

"I've loved him since I was twelve. We made love for the first time a few months ago, when he came back home after five years. He's been home since August, telling me he loved me, and he just told me he's engaged to someone else. He's been lying to me for months."

Linc took a deep breath. "Wow. And so you're here with me." He said this sadly.

She pulled away, wiping her face. "I've liked you since the night we met," she admitted.

He looked uncomfortable. "Me, too. But I don't have a girlfriend."

"Well, I don't have a boyfriend anymore."

"What if Patrick drops his fiancée? What if he begs you to forgive him and take him back?"

"I don't know if what he does matters anymore. He was my best friend. And I don't want to think about him right now."

She leaned over and kissed his neck, pressing her lips against his skin and letting her hands spread against his chest. She felt him resist at first, then pull her to him. This time she was lost in the way the muscles in his back felt against her hands, the way he rolled over and pulled her on top of him, the way his fingers tangled in her hair as he whispered her name over and over. This time she didn't see anything from afar, didn't observe herself performing a rebound ritual. This time her entire body shivered, and when it was done, she couldn't think. She fell asleep with her back curved against him, his arm across her hip, his breath against her neck.

Chapter 11

The next morning, Wednesday, Katrina awoke before Linc and slipped out of bed without waking him. He lay on his stomach, his breathing slow and rhythmic. She thought it was a good thing he didn't snore—that would drive her crazy. But she felt odd even thinking that. Did it matter whether he snored? Would there be other mornings when she woke up next to him? She glanced at him while she slipped on a T-shirt and sweatpants. He looked much younger while asleep. Innocent. She closed the bedroom door behind her and went out to the living room.

She stepped to the bay window. It was already sunny and bright, one of those days that looked like summer, fooled you into thinking it was warm, then surprised you with its frosty bite. She stepped out quickly to get the paper. The air smelled sweet and cold like the winter Saturdays when she was a child, when she would get up at the first sign of light, don her snowsuit and spend the day playing and running and laughing. The grass was still stiff with frost, and she wondered if it would snow in time for the holidays.

Closing the door behind her, she instantly decided not to go to work. She called and left another message, this time saying that she wasn't coming in for the rest of the week. She was due a little vacation, anyway. If they thought she was sick, maybe it would stop them from calling to see where she'd put the Mackenzie file, whom they should call for proofs on the latest ads. It could wait.

She glanced at the clock. 8:30. What time would Linc awaken? He must sleep late, she supposed, since he worked late. Did he work every night? He'd said he didn't have a girlfriend, but was there someone else who would wonder why he hadn't come home last night? A roommate?

She quietly prepared a cup of peppermint tea and sat down on the sofa, her sock-clad feet propped on the coffee table. Katrina thought about how much Linc had told her about himself at the party, and how little she still knew about him. It was odd, having him here, sleeping in the next room. It wasn't that she had never had spur-of-the moment sex, something unpremeditated and often ill-advised, physical contact to numb the senses. But she never spent the night with those guys. She never brought them to her apartment, never let them throw their arms over her while they slept, never wondered who might be waiting at home for them. That Linc was here and she was waiting for him to awaken was enough to make her uneasy. She suddenly wished she'd gone to his place, so she could be gone by now, not worried about what they would say to each other under the shine of daylight and reason.

"What are you thinking about?" She was startled to hear his voice behind her. He wore his clothes from the night before, his shirt untucked, feet bare. His five o'clock shadow was darker this morning, and his thick eyebrows were mussed. In spite of herself, she was charmed by his morning disarray.

"How do you know I was thinking? Maybe I was just sitting here enjoying a cup of tea," she said, smiling slightly as he plopped down on the couch beside her.

He shook his head. "Nope, I saw you staring poetically out the window. You were definitely thinking."

"I guess I was thinking about you. Want some tea?"

"I don't drink caffeine. What about me?"

No caffeine? How did he manage to stay up all night with no caffeine? One more thing she didn't know.

"I was just thinking about how much I don't know about you."

He considered this. "We don't know a lot of things about each other, actually. But what we do know is pretty important."

She looked at him. "Like what?"

"Well, we've gotten the eighties duo question out of the way. We know neither of us snores. And we both think there could be something happening between us."

He was only half-serious, but even half was too much for her right now. She tried to lighten the mood. "*Something* already happened," she joked.

"Something real, I mean." He waited to see what her reaction would be.

She averted her eyes, reached for her tea. "Linc."

He held up a hand. "I know, you just got out of a relationship. You might even still be in a relationship. You have no idea what's going to happen. You're still too upset about the Patrick thing to deal with a new relationship. You aren't ready for anything serious," he rattled off.

She shrugged. "All of that is true."

"I know. But I'm not that easily discouraged."

She looked down into her cup. "I don't want to mislead you, though."

"I'm a big boy. I can take care of myself."

She didn't want to have this conversation. She didn't want to have to make excuses for her confusion. "I'm not sure this was a good idea."

Linc looked annoyed. "Just for the record, I asked you about that before I came in here last night."

"I told you I didn't know."

"So, fine, whatever. It happened, and I'm not sorry." He stood up. "Do you have any juice?"

She frowned. "In the fridge. And I didn't say I was *sorry*."

She listened to him searching through the cabinets for a glass. He paused in the doorway before pouring the juice. "Then what are you saying?"

She wasn't sure *what* she was saying. "I'm just really upset right now, and confused. I don't want to get into a rebound relationship because I'm mad at Patrick."

Linc stood in the doorway to the kitchen holding a full glass of orange juice. "Look, I like you a lot. But it doesn't have to be a big thing if you don't want it to be."

"Do you want it to be?" She already knew the answer to that. She was pretty sure he did want it to be a big thing. Or at least something that wasn't simple and easy.

He looked uncomfortable and took a sip of juice. "Does it matter what I want?"

"That's not an answer."

He shrugged and came into the living room but sat in the chair so he could see her face. "So are you going to call Patrick?"

Now it was her turn to be annoyed. She wished he would stop talking about Patrick, stop trying to force her to say more about it than she already had. She didn't know where last night fit into her life, and in a way, she resented his asking. Letting Linc see her naked didn't give him the right to psychoanalyze her, did it?

"Why should I call him?" Her voice rose.

He raised both eyebrows but seemed unaffected by her anger. "Unfinished business."

She sighed, exasperated. "He's engaged. It's finished."

He looked at her steadily. "If it were finished, I wouldn't be here this morning."

She shook her head. "I don't want to talk about it."

He went on as if she hadn't spoken. "Yeah, there's an attraction between us. But weren't you attracted to me a few days ago? We didn't have sex then."

She frowned and picked at lint on her college sweatpants. The block letters that spelled out *Illinois* were cracked and fading after years of wear. "Don't spoil this, okay? Don't make this about Patrick."

He leaned forward in his chair. "It already *is* about him, and you know it. That's why you should talk to him."

She rolled her eyes. "And say what?"

He waved a hand in the air. "Whatever. But it doesn't seem right to let a fifteen-year friendship go down the tubes without at least yelling at him a little."

She smiled in spite of herself. Linc had a way of catching her off guard, and she found it difficult to maintain her irritation with him. "How do you know I didn't already yell at him?"

"I've been on the wrong end of enough bad breakups to know the signs. You're trying to pretend like you're fine, and you're not."

"You sound like Chrissy. And instead of quizzing me about Patrick, why don't you tell me about all these bad breakups?"

"Maybe some other time."

Katrina felt as if something had been settled, although she wasn't sure what. She stood up.

"Well. I better get dressed."

He glanced at his watch. "Isn't it late? I figured you were taking the day off."

He looked at her, hopeful, and she felt guilty.

He caught the expression on her face and looked away. "If you want me to leave, I'll go. I'm not an idiot, and I don't want to be here if you don't want me here."

Katrina felt terrible. "I just don't want things to get any weirder than they already are."

He stood and looked into her eyes. "Things are not weird. We're just talking."

"It feels weird to me." She felt trapped. No matter what she did, the conversation would not ease into the light, amicable exchange she craved. Even her clumsy attempt to send Linc away had backfired and she could see that he was a little hurt. She wanted to make it up to him.

"Whatever. I'm going to go get dressed," he said and moved toward the bedroom.

She touched his shoulder as he passed her. "Wait. I'm sorry. This is all really new to me, you know? I haven't dated anyone seriously, since, well, I never have, really. Other than Patrick." The words, too revealing and raw, came out with difficulty.

"What does that have to do with me leaving?"

She saw that he wasn't going to make her apology an easy one. "Other guys that I've slept with—they never stayed over. And if they did, we both agreed it was a good idea for them to get out as soon as possible in the morning. You're different."

He softened. "I don't know."

"Want some breakfast? Maybe we could just eat and not talk about the heavy stuff for a while," she said quickly. She didn't want him to disappear; she only wanted him to stop making it harder for her to pretend that her feelings weren't jumbled like a bag of old clothes on their way to Goodwill.

He walked over to her, put his hands on her cheeks and stared down at her gently. "Are you going to call him?"

"I'll think about it." She wasn't interested in talking to Patrick, but she would have said virtually anything to change the subject.

"Good. And maybe after you talk to him, we can make plans."

"For what?"

"Our first date. Now, I like my eggs over easy, and can I use the shower?"

She laughed. The idea of a date with Linc was intriguing, even though it seemed a little like going backward after last night, after this morning. "Don't get used to me making you breakfast, and the towels are in the hall closet."

He leaned down and kissed her lightly on the lips before stepping toward the bedroom. "Thanks. Remember, *over easy,*" he teased.

She pretended to throw her cup at him as he playfully ducked his way out of the room.

Katrina settled into a more temperate mood as she tried to cook Linc's eggs over easy, messed them up and decided he'd have to live with scrambled, which was how *she* liked them. Cooking relaxed her as long as no one was forcing her to do it. When the eggs started to sizzle, she added chopped red pepper and onions, salt and coarse black pepper. She cut up some oranges and grapefruit, and she toasted cinnamon raisin bagels for them.

She stood over the toaster and breathed in. She loved the smell of burning crumbs combined with the murky sweetness of warming raisins. Her parents used to laugh at her, bending over the toaster, once singeing the tip of her nose when she got too close. But she didn't care. The fragrance was irresistible.

As she scooped eggs onto plates, she heard the shower stop. Soon Linc emerged, beads of water still dripping from his smooth head, jeans loose around his waist, shirtless. Katrina felt a little shy, seeing him like this. Half-dressed, he seemed more naked than he had last night.

"Do you want your sweater?" she asked, busying herself with setting the small breakfast table.

"What sweater?" He made a move toward her. "Can I help with anything?"

She shook her head. "The one I borrowed the other night."

He laughed and sat down. "Oh, yeah, the one I let you keep so I could make up an excuse to come back."

She smiled. "So you planned all this?"

"How could I? You're the one who came to the club. Maybe *you* planned it," he teased, transferring a mound of eggs, sliced orange and a bagel to his plate.

"Yeah, right." She sat across from him and helped herself. "So are you putting on the sweater or what? It's in my top dresser drawer if you want it."

"Why should I?" He chewed and swallowed. "Great eggs. Not over easy, but I like scrambled, too."

"It's distracting."

"What?"

"You sitting around with no shirt on."

Before they could continue, she heard a car drive up, a door slam. She'd spent her childhood listening to the sound of her mother's loafers clicking on the sidewalk outside the door, so before the doorbell even rang she knew it was Annie. She put her head in her hands.

"What's wrong?" Linc stopped eating, alarmed.

"It's my mom."

"What's your mom?" He looked around the apartment quickly.

"Outside. My mom."

He stood up. "How do you know?"

"Trust me. I know the sound of her footsteps."

"Uh oh." They listened to the doorbell, frozen in their places, looking at each other.

Annie rang the bell again, then knocked loudly on the door. Painfully aware of Linc's bare chest, Katrina trudged to the door.

"Hi, honey." Annie stepped inside briskly. She leaned over and kissed Katrina on the cheek, then noticed Linc, who was standing near his unfinished plate of food.

Annie seemed to be the only one in the room not at a loss for words. She smiled brightly at Linc and walked over to him with her hand extended. "Hi, I'm Katrina's mother, Annie. I don't think we've met."

Linc retreated from his horrified stupor long enough to respond.

"Hi, I'm Linc Davis. How are you?" He smiled as brightly as Annie, and Katrina wondered why she couldn't seem to manufacture one of these smiles that helped distract them all from the fact that her mother had just walked in on Katrina with a half-naked man who was not Patrick.

They stood there smiling at each other silently while Katrina searched for words.

Finally, Linc made a yawning motion, which Katrina wondered about, but it seemed to work as a transition.

"Well, I guess I'll go get dressed. I have a bunch of errands to do before work. Need to get going," he stuttered, nodding at Annie, flashing a look of alarm at Katrina before leaving the room. She heard him opening drawers and gathering up his stuff.

Annie turned to Katrina, her eyes narrowed. "He seems like a nice young man."

Katrina cleared her throat. "Want some tea?"

"No thanks," Annie said pleasantly, planting herself firmly on the sofa. She looked at Katrina expectantly.

Before Annie's silence became too heavy for Katrina to bear, Linc came out of the bedroom. He wore his gray sweater and he was buttoning his pea coat as he moved toward the door.

"Well, it was nice meeting you, Mrs. Larson. Katrina, I'll talk to you soon?"

She nodded and walked him to the door. She felt bad that he had to leave without saying anything more than that, but she couldn't imagine a thing more embarrassing than having an intimate conversation with Linc in front of her mother.

"I'll call you later. Or you call me," he said on his way out the door. She nodded quickly, both relieved and sorry he was gone.

Katrina wished she could stand in the doorway forever, but it was cold, and her mother's eyes bored a hole in the back of her scalp, so she closed the door and plopped down on the chair Linc had occupied earlier.

"Mom, what are you doing here?" Katrina brushed her hands over her wildly curling hair, hoping desperately that, for once, her mother might decide to let her get away with something. She tried to look as if nothing was amiss.

Annie eyed her up and down. "I was at Charles's last night, and I thought I'd have breakfast with you. Called you at work—they said you were sick. So I dropped by."

Annie followed Katrina into the kitchen, where she began to make a new pot of tea.

"You're sleeping with Charles?" Katrina asked petulantly, covering her embarrassment with anger.

Annie narrowed her eyes, and Katrina immediately knew that she'd gone too far.

"Not that I have to answer to you, but yes. I'm sleeping with Charles. And who are *you* sleeping with?" She nodded toward the door out of which Linc had made his exit.

Katrina sighed, grabbing mugs out of the cabinet. "I don't want to get into it."

"Oh, I'm sure you'd rather get into my personal business than talk about yours. Where's Patrick?"

"I don't know. I don't care."

Annie grabbed Katrina's hand, stopping her from going to the refrigerator for milk and lemon.

"What's wrong with you? You're not sick, I see, so tell me what's going on."

Katrina abandoned the tea preparations and sat down at the round wooden table.

"Don't you have to go to work?"

Annie got angry. "Stop being a brat and tell me what's wrong, who's that young man I just met, and what's going on with you and Patrick."

Katrina reluctantly told her about Patrick's engagement and provided only the barest details about Vinyl and Linc. Annie fumed visibly about Patrick, and Katrina could see the restraint it took for her mother not to demand more information about Linc. But rather than spew questions, her mother sat and listened. Even though Katrina had resisted this, it felt good to get it all out, to talk to the only person who might understand.

"It's not so much that he's engaged. I mean, I hate that, but I could have dealt with him being in love with someone else. So, fine, he should marry her if he loves her. But that he lied to me for months since he's been back—years before that, actually, since he never once mentioned even that Jamie was a woman."

Annie nodded sympathetically. "I know that feeling. I went through something like this with your dad, except it wasn't another woman. Another woman might have been easier to take, but the fact that he just didn't want to be married to me anymore and that he hid it for God knows how long—well, it was hard."

Katrina was surprised. "I didn't know that's how it was with you and Daddy."

"That's exactly how it was. For so long I went along thinking everything was fine. Not perfect, but we were getting along. Then one day he disappears, leaving a note that says he's not happy. It was like he let me live a lie."

Katrina thought about this for a while. "It sounds dumb, naïve, but I always thought that Daddy would come back someday. I thought he might sweep in here with a reasonable explanation for where he's been all these years, and we'd be closer than ever."

Annie smiled sadly. "I thought something like that, too, for a long time. Only in my fairy tale, he would explain why he didn't love me enough to stay and try to make things good again."

Annie dug a tissue out of her purse and handed it to Katrina, who had begun rubbing her eyes with the tips of her fingers. She stood and put her arm around Katrina's shoulders. "You know, sometimes you have to let go of what was and find something new to be happy about."

"Mom, I just found out about Jamie and Patrick. How can you expect me to let go, suddenly be okay with this whole thing?" Katrina looked up at her mother and squeezed the tissue, dabbing at the corners of her eyes and trying not to lose control. She was tired of crying. What good was it doing? She looked away, trying to stop her eyes from watering.

"Now, that's not what I said," Annie scolded. "You've been holding on to this idea that you and Patrick were meant to be since you were a girl. Right?"

Katrina refused to look at her mother. "I never said that."

"But it's true. And all I'm saying is, what if that's your fairy tale? What if you considered the possibility that he doesn't love you the way you've always loved him?"

Katrina felt lost. "Loving Patrick is a part of me, Mom. How can I just let it go, just like that?"

Annie shook her head. "It doesn't happen 'just like that.' But you have to start somewhere. Not necessarily by sleeping with another man, not by refusing to talk about it, but by telling yourself it's okay for big girls to let go of fairy tales."

They were quiet. Katrina was light-headed. She needed to eat more than just the couple of mouthfuls of eggs and the slice of orange she'd managed to get down before her mother came. She needed something to make her feel more grounded. She sighed heavily.

"I don't know how to do that."

Annie looked her in the eye. "Talk to Patrick."

All the people in her life were starting to sound the same. Chrissy. Linc. Her mother. "I thought you just said to try to move on."

"Katrina, he's been your best friend for years and years. You can't just let your friendship go without talking. I'm not telling you to forgive him. I'm not telling you to listen to his excuses. But you need to tell him how *you* feel."

"I don't know if I can do that."

"You have to." Annie looked at her watch reluctantly. "Honey, I have to get to work, and driving back to Madison in traffic will take awhile." She gathered up her purse and coat. "And you should get out, too. Don't sit around here feeling sorry for yourself. Go to the gym or something. Think about what I said," Annie ordered sweetly.

Katrina stood up and hugged her mother. "I love you."

Annie squeezed her tightly. "You're my baby girl. I have to take care of you. Now go get dressed."

Katrina laughed and wiped her eyes. "I'm going, I'm going."

Chapter 12

On the day Annie scared Linc away, Chrissy called just after Katrina had gotten back from doing forty-five minutes on the treadmill. She had considered not answering the phone, but she finally picked it up on the fourth ring.

"It took you long enough to answer." By the determined tone in Chrissy's voice, not to mention the impatient greeting, Katrina knew she wouldn't be able to brush off her best friend with a refusal to talk about Linc or Patrick.

"Hi." Katrina spread her towel down on the overstuffed living room chair before flopping down.

"So?"

Katrina didn't reply, taking one last chance at stonewalling Chrissy. Chrissy waited, playing that old game of verbal chicken that Annie used so effectively. Pose a question that Katrina didn't want to answer, then challenge her to stay quiet. Katrina always blinked first.

"So. You want to know about last night."

Chrissy tsked. "No, I was wondering what's on Oprah today."

"Sarcasm. Cute." Katrina untied her shoes and leaned over to peel them off. "Where do you want me to start?"

"Hmm. Maybe the moment after you practically shoved me into a cab at Vinyl? Did Linc give you a ride home? Did anything happen?"

She wanted to lie. Wanted to say, "He took me home, we said good night and that was it." Or maybe she'd stick in a sweet kiss at the door for good measure.

But part of her *wanted* to tell Chrissy. Maybe Chrissy could say something that would make her confusion melt away. Maybe she would know why Katrina felt both excited and nervous remembering how she and Linc had lain in each other's arms last night.

"He took me home."

"And? He left, right? He's a nice guy; he wouldn't try to take advantage of a woman like that," Chrissy said knowingly.

"What do you mean, 'take advantage'? I'm a big girl, not some little weakling who doesn't know what she's doing," she said, annoyed.

"Whoa, I never said you were a weakling. I just meant that if you told him about Patrick—"

"What makes you think I told him about Patrick?"

"Did you?"

"That's not the point."

Chrissy sighed. "Look, all I'm trying to say is that Linc's a nice guy and he likes you." She paused. "Why are you getting so upset about some stupid thing I blurted out anyway?"

Katrina shook her head. She could almost hear Chrissy making mental connections in the brief silence.

"You slept with him, didn't you?"

"Okay, one minute you're talking about how Linc would never do that, and now you're saying he did."

"You did, didn't you? You slept with him!"

Katrina's weak denial was drowned out by Chrissy's laughter.

"Why is that funny?"

"It's not, really. I mean, it's funny that you tried to hide it from me with this rampage about a poor choice of words," Chrissy said, still chuckling. "But seriously, I can't believe you did that."

"Why not? People have sex all the time. It's no big deal."

Chrissy snorted. "No big deal? You find out on Monday your boyfriend has been lying to you for months and is *engaged* to another woman. On Tuesday you sit around all day in your pajamas, then you go out to a club and have sex with the bartender. That's no big deal?"

"Oh come on, it's not like I picked up some random bartender. I already knew Linc, remember? You wanted to fix me up with him a few days ago."

"I wanted you two to hang out, maybe see a movie or go out to eat. I never suggested you sleep together!"

Katrina was silent, unwilling to defend herself.

"What about Patrick?"

"What about him?"

"Did you talk to Linc about what happened?"

"Who talks about her ex-boyfriend while she's having sex with another man?"

"Did you?" Chrissy pressed.

Katrina sighed. "Some."

"What did Linc say?"

"Not much. He's worried that I was doing it to get back at Patrick, and—" She stopped herself. She didn't want to go on. It was too intimate, too personal. "Why am I telling you all this? You're so nosy, just like my mother."

"I'm only trying to understand all this. You can't blame me for that, right? You're my best friend." Chrissy changed her tack. "So how was it?"

Now Katrina laughed. "You've got a lot of nerve, you know that?"

"It was good, wasn't it?"

Katrina thought about that first time, the way she'd seduced him, the way she couldn't quite relax. She thought about the second time, when she'd forgotten all about making the right moves, when all she could think of was the way his hands felt light and soft against her skin. Did all that add up to *good?*

"It was interesting," she said.

"Interesting?"

"Yes." Katrina hoped that Chrissy caught the caution in her voice. She wasn't going to talk about the taste of Linc's skin or the sounds he'd made. They'd shared those details about their partners many times before, but this time it didn't seem quite right. Plus, it's not like Chrissy was telling her any of this stuff about Rick, a point that Katrina kept to herself lest Chrissy offer details she'd rather not hear in expectation of quid pro quo.

"So I guess badgering you for more information would be useless?" Chrissy asked hopefully.

"I've already told you too much."

"But we're best friends. We tell each other everything," Chrissy said.

Katrina laughed, and after a moment Chrissy joined her. They both knew that even best friends didn't tell each other *everything*.

"Okay, okay, I give up. Just one more thing—are you going to see Linc again?"

Katrina rubbed her temples. Lately people were always asking her questions, and she didn't have adequate answers. Would she see him again? Probably. At the club, or at another of Chrissy's parties, or maybe during a chance meeting at the mall. Would she date him? Katrina wasn't sure how she felt about that. One the one hand, he was an interesting, caring guy with a great body. On the other hand, the last thing she needed was another entanglement. But she didn't want to discuss it with Chrissy.

"My mom came over this morning while Linc was running

around half-naked," she said instead.

"Oh my God! Did they meet?" Chrissy loved to hear about intrigue like this.

"Unfortunately, yes. By the time we picked our jaws up off the floor, she was ringing the front doorbell."

Chrissy laughed in anticipation. "I bet Annie's expression was priceless. What did she say?"

"You know my mom. She can play anything cool. She just introduced herself and smiled like nothing was happening. Then he went to put on a shirt and grab his stuff, while I'm left trying to pretend this is all normal."

"Did she know about Patrick?"

"She does now." Katrina shook her head, thinking about how uncomfortable things had been. "He couldn't wait to get out of here."

"Can't blame him." The amusement in Chrissy's voice died down. "Of course, you didn't answer my question."

Katrina sighed. "What?"

"Are you going to see Linc again or not?" Chrissy repeated patiently.

"He said he'd call me."

"And when he does?"

"*If* he does, we'll go from there." Katrina wasn't sure what "going from there" would entail, so she opted not to elaborate.

"Uh-huh. Well, some of us have to work, so I've got to go. Hey, why don't you come out to dinner with me and Rick tomorrow?"

Katrina cleared her throat. "Oh, no, I don't think so."

"You have to eat," Chrissy insisted.

"I'll order pizza."

"Katrina."

"Talk to you later Chris." She hung up the phone before Chrissy could wear down her defenses.

★ ★ ★ ★ ★

For the next two weeks Katrina worked until eight every evening and went to the gym after that. She talked to her mom a lot, nearly once a day. Not about Patrick or Linc or even Charles, really. She just liked the sound of Annie's good-natured complaining about the kids she treated at school, about the lack of snow for the upcoming holidays, about the price of fresh turkeys. She talked often to Chrissy, too, although Chrissy was adamant about trying to talk about things Katrina wanted to pretend didn't exist. She'd managed to convince Chrissy that asking about Linc all the time was annoying. But she couldn't stop Chrissy from inviting her on all sorts of outings with Rick.

"I don't want to be a fifth wheel," Katrina would say.

"You know we don't think of you that way," Chrissy would counter.

"But I'd feel like I was horning in on your date," Katrina would repeat.

"So bring Linc." Chrissy saved this trump card for the end of the conversation when it was clear that Katrina could not be persuaded. They both knew it was coming, but it was like they were performing a script that was etched onto the smooth side of a stone.

And as the script dictated, Katrina would refuse and tell Chrissy she'd talk to her in a couple of days, giving them time to rehearse their parts before replaying the whole thing over again.

Katrina never gave a clear reason why she didn't invite Linc, because she didn't know. The fact was, she hadn't spoken to Linc in two weeks, since the morning he'd escaped her mother's probing gaze.

Naturally, he'd called. And called. And called. His answering machine messages, every one of which she'd saved, charted the course of his feelings over the past 14 days. The first couple of days his voice was mild and pleasant, hopeful that she would call him back, sure she was simply busy. The next few days she detected a note of worry in the way he cleared his throat and spoke too fast. After that he stopped calling so often, trickling down to once in the last week. His final message, left three days ago, was simple and brief, and instead of the anger she expected, he just sounded resigned.

"Katrina, I don't know why you haven't called me back. Or maybe I do. Anyway, I'm not going to leave any more messages. When you're ready to talk to me, call me. Bye."

She wasn't ready, not yet, and she didn't know why. She liked the fact that he'd called so often, and she nursed the small voice in her mind whispering that Patrick hadn't called, or if he had, he hadn't left a message and that was just as good as not calling at all. But a part of her still held back, and she couldn't bring herself to return Linc's calls.

Instead, she buried herself in writing catchy ads for cough syrup and trying to achieve her optimal heart rate. She felt bad about not calling him back. He might think he'd done something wrong or that she had used him. And she didn't think that was true. It was easier to come home exhausted every day, check the answering machine and plop down on the sofa with a thick book until she fell asleep still wearing her clothes, the glasses she wore for reading lying crooked on her face.

Tonight she came home later than usual after a long meeting where her bosses decided that her copy was too "downbeat." She checked the silent answering machine and showered quickly, ready to resume her place on the sofa. As she pulled back the shower curtain with one hand, squeezing water out of her hair with the other, the phone rang into the silence of the apartment. It was already 10:30, and Katrina wondered who was calling her so late.

"Hello?"

"So you are alive."

Linc. Katrina felt embarrassed and nervous and pleased all at once. Now she would have to try to make excuses for her poor behavior. Still, the sound of his voice immediately lifted her mood.

"Hey." Katrina looked down and realized the water rolling from her skin was creating a wet spot on the beige carpet. She sat down on the bed and finished drying off. Rubbing her calves, she couldn't think of anything that would adequately explain the fact that she hadn't called him back. She briefly wished that she really didn't want to talk to him. But she did, so she tried to draw him out.

"How are you? Been working a lot?" She said it sweetly, trying to pretend like everything was normal, whatever that meant for them.

"You think I'm mad, don't you?" She thought she heard a smile.

"Yeah, but I was trying not to be obvious about it," she sighed. "So are you?"

He was quiet for a moment. "Well, I don't know if *mad* is the right word. Disappointed. Worried. Maybe a little annoyed. But not really mad." He was teasing, but she heard the truth behind his words.

"I'm sorry. I was, well, I don't know what, really. Okay, this is not helping." She stumbled to find the words to describe the confusion she'd felt for the past two weeks.

He laughed. "You're right. It's not helping."

"I know. But the 'sorry' part—I really mean that."

"I understand. Or at least I think I do. That's why I called." His voice was soft and disarming.

She spread her towel underneath her on the bed and laid back. "You said on your last message that you weren't going to call again," she said quietly.

"I couldn't help it. I thought if I could catch you, I would just tell you that it's okay."

"What's okay?"

"That you don't want to talk. I felt bad for trying to make you talk about things when I was there. I shouldn't have pushed you. I shouldn't have called you so much. So I called to say it's okay. And to apologize."

Katrina closed her eyes and smiled. How could he be this nice? "I can't believe you're apologizing after I didn't return even one of your calls."

He laughed. "I only called nine times. Maybe you just didn't have a chance to get back to me."

Eight times, she mentally corrected him. "Yeah, you have to call at least ten times to get an answer from me."

"Ah, so close."

They were silent, each waiting for the other to speak.

"So, were you in the middle of something when I called?" Linc said finally.

"Just got out of the shower," she said without thinking. Then, realizing she was naked, she felt exposed, even though they were miles apart.

"Oh." He cleared his throat.

She wondered what that meant. "Oh" as in "Who cares?" "Oh" as in "I'm picturing you naked right now"? This time the quiet was uncomfortable, so she tried to fix it.

"I didn't say that to be sexy or provocative or anything. I really did just get out of the shower."

He cleared his throat again. Maybe he could use some of the cough syrup she'd been trying to hawk for the past few weeks. "Showering this late at night?"

She wished they could get off the subject of her nakedness. "I was at the gym."

"Oh." There it was again.

She laughed nervously. "This conversation sure took a turn for the worse."

He gave a dry chuckle similar to hers. "I think it was the shower thing. It's distracting."

"Yeah, well, it's getting late. Maybe I should go."

"Yeah, I understand. I just wanted to call and say, you know, sorry," he said.

"I'm glad you called."

"Me, too." He paused. "Can I press my luck and ask you something?" He went ahead before she could answer. "Can I see you? I promise we don't have to get into anything heavy. I just like hanging out with you," he said quickly, as if he was afraid she would say no. "Maybe Chrissy and Rick would want to come, too."

Katrina thought maybe she should say no, maybe she should stop trying to pretend nothing was wrong and deal with whatever it was she was feeling. But she wanted to see Linc. She'd liked hanging out with him, too. Plus, shouldn't she make amends for the unreturned phone calls?

"What are you doing tomorrow night?" She didn't know what Chrissy had planned, but she had a feeling this new Linc development would take precedence. "Oh, wait, it's Friday. You're probably working," she said.

"Nope, I've got the weekend off. See you tomorrow."

"Linc?" She stopped. She wanted to say something to let him know that the thought of him brought a smile to her face. But she didn't. Couldn't.

"Yeah?"

"Good night."

Katrina was exhausted, but as soon as she got into bed she

immediately began to obsess about seeing Linc tomorrow. What should she wear? Where would they go? Was this a good idea? Maybe something black, not too sexy. Or should she go to Marshall Fields during lunch and find something sexy? He'd said he liked her in red. But she wasn't comfortable in red.

After half an hour, she'd worked herself up into a panic. She didn't want him to think that since they'd spent the night together, that meant she wanted to repeat the experience. Well, she might want to repeat it, but maybe not right away. Katrina glanced at the clock. 11:30. Too late to call Chrissy? She picked up the phone and dialed.

"Yeah?" Chrissy's voice was scratchy and low. She'd definitely been sleeping.

"Are you asleep?"

"Katrina?"

"If you're sleeping, I can call to you tomorrow," she said quickly. She crossed her fingers and hoped that Chrissy would talk to her.

There was a rustling, and the phone made a loud clanking noise in Katrina's ear. Chrissy had dropped the phone.

"Chrissy?"

"I'm here. Sorry." Chrissy paused groggily, and Katrina worried that Chrissy had fallen back asleep. Chrissy finally cleared her throat.

"What's wrong?" Her voice was beginning to clear.

"I have a date with Linc tomorrow. Actually, we have a double date. With you and Rick."

"What?" Already Chrissy was more alert.

"Linc. Date. Tomorrow. And I'm freaking out."

"Since when do you—we—have a date with him? I just talked to you a couple of days ago."

"I have no idea what to wear, where we're going, whether I

should suggest somewhere or let him plan it."

"Wait a second. Why are you so worked up? You're acting like you've never been out on a date before," Chrissy said.

Katrina frowned, not knowing exactly why she was so unnerved. "He suggested that maybe you and Rick might want to come along. You don't have to."

Chrissy sounded wide awake now. "Calm down. Of course I'll go. I wouldn't miss it, actually."

Katrina kept talking. "I know it shouldn't be a big deal, but it is. I don't know why. Patrick and I weren't really dating, not like this. We were friends, then, well, you know." Her voice quieted and she was sorry she'd brought up Patrick.

"Speaking of Patrick—" Chrissy said quickly.

"Please don't. We're talking about Linc here."

Chrissy sighed. "You know, at some point you're going to have to do something about the whole Patrick thing."

She closed her eyes. She knew Chrissy was right, and her friend's words pushed air into the little balloon of doubt floating in her thoughts. She needed to do something about the Patrick situation, although she wasn't quite sure what. But not now. Not yet.

"Do you think I should wear black?"

"What?"

"Are you falling asleep again? Should I wear black tomorrow, with Linc?"

Chrissy was silent for a moment. "What about the black pants suit you bought last year?"

She let the air out of her lungs in relief. "Thanks, Chrissy."

She heard Chrissy sigh again. "So, what about your hair?"

Chapter 13

Katrina tried to convince Linc that they should meet Chrissy and Rick at the restaurant. There would be less pressure, less pre-meal chatter that way. Less chance for him to flash his crooked smile at her. Less chance for her to be distracted by the way he smelled—just the slightest hint of a woodsy cologne that you had to be really close to detect.

But he said no, it was a date, and people on dates go places together.

"But we'll be together once we get to the restaurant," she said reasonably, hoping he wouldn't think she was being a snob. She'd called him during her lunch hour on Friday while she picked at a turkey and Swiss sandwich from Cousins.

"I'll pick you up."

She pushed the excess cheese around her plate and thought about sitting in her apartment, waiting for Linc to arrive, constantly checking and rechecking herself in the mirror. "Why don't I drive instead?"

He laughed. "Don't want to ride in the Honda, huh?"

"Well, it is kind of old," she teased.

"I had no idea Her Majesty required a chariot." He said this in a terrible English accent that made her smile.

"Seriously, you've driven me home a couple of times. Let me return the favor."

She realized after they hung up that she would be seeing his place for the first time. Now, she'd find out if he had a girlfriend lurking in the recent past. He'd said he wasn't involved with anyone, but if she spotted a Pottery Barn catalog or a set of matching pasta bowls, she'd know there had been someone.

Katrina dressed carefully. She set the shower as hot as she could stand it and smoothed on Chanel No. 5 body lotion afterward. She brushed her hair until the curls turned into waves that she drew into a chignon at the nape of her neck. A few pieces of blue lint stuck to her black pants, and she picked them off before dressing. Thinking that a button-down shirt would be too nine-to-five for a Friday night, she abandoned the idea of a shirt altogether and put on the tailored jacket over her black lace bra. She buttoned the jacket until just a hint of the tops of her breasts showed. Gold stud earrings, a bracelet her mother had given her, a touch of lipstick and mascara. Turning in front of the mirror, Katrina examined herself critically. Too much cleavage? She glanced at her watch and realized that, too much or not, it was time to go.

Linc lived on the bottom floor of a duplex on the East side, near the university. The street was lined with old oak trees, their branches bare in anticipation of the winter's snow, but she could imagine their leaves shading the street into near darkness on a summer day. These were the kinds of streets she'd loved as a child. The house she'd lived in with her parents was in a newer neighborhood on the Northwest side, where the trees had been adolescent and didn't provide much shade at all. She'd always thought that when she grew up, she'd live in a house surrounded by oaks and maples, and she'd make her kids rake the lawn in the fall and push an old manual lawn mower around in the summer, and they'd love it because *she* had loved that sort of thing as a kid.

She circled around the block a couple of times before she found a parking spot. She twisted the rearview mirror to check her face one last time. As she walked along the sidewalk leading to his house, she noticed that the lawn was neatly mowed, although it was starting to turn brown from the cold. The house was a two-story wood frame, painted white with coral trim. Pine hedges framed the large front window, and wind chimes made of bamboo whistles hung next to the door.

Linc opened the door before she could ring the bell.

"Hey," he smiled at her. He wore khaki pants and a white shirt, a brown blazer with a subtle hounds-tooth pattern just a shade darker than his skin. His face was freshly shaved, and he even wore a tie. He looked comfortable, even though he had once told her he hated to dress up. She had the feeling he was comfortable in anything, really. This was a different side of him, a side that she liked, but she tried to play it cool walking in the door.

"Hey." He took her coat and, as she walked over to the sofa, she felt him looking her up and down. He hovered near her as she sat on the edge of the couch. She ran her hand over her hair quickly, hoping she looked okay.

"Something to drink before we go?" He tapped his foot on the carpet nervously.

"Sure. I think we have time before dinner."

He nodded and disappeared into the kitchen.

Katrina looked around while she waited. The living room was painted a deep, muted gold accented with white trim. The room was large, furnished simply with an unfinished wooden coffee table, an off-white loveseat and sofa and an antique rocker. The walls were decorated with movie posters in thick black frames. *The Godfather. Do the Right Thing. The Usual Suspects. Lady Sings the Blues.* The room was neat but not obsessively so—she spotted a pair of his boots in the corner behind the door and saw an unruly pile of books on the small table near the entryway.

He came back into the room juggling two bottles of Amstel

Light and tall, narrow glasses. He set them down on the table and sat on the sofa next to her.

"You didn't even ask me what I wanted," she teased.

He was horrified. "Oh, God, I'm so sorry!" He looked at the bottles. "Is beer okay? I can't believe I did that." He shook his head.

She laughed. "It's fine, really. I like Amstel Light. Really, I love it. It's the only beer I drink. Actually, it's the only beverage I drink, period. In the morning, I gargle with it." She was relieved that he'd made the first dumb move. It made whatever she might do or say wrong, which she felt was sure to happen, potentially less embarrassing.

He laughed and shook his head. "You're sweet to try to make me feel better, but that was so dumb."

"More like presumptuous, really," she teased.

"Hey, I thought we were trying to make me feel better here."

"Oh, right."

They both relaxed a little while he poured the beers expertly and handed her a glass.

"So." He sipped and glanced over at her.

"So. How did you get the night off? I figured you must work pretty much every weekend," she said. She hated small talk, because she was usually so bad at it. But she wanted to stick to the traditionally safe topics, work being the only one she could think of at the moment.

"We alternate weekends so no one gets burned out. But I think I'm getting tired of it anyway." He sat back on his end of the sofa and turned slightly so he was facing her.

"When we talked at the party you said you were thinking about what to do next." She relaxed a bit and modeled her sitting position after his. She took a sip of her beer, which was actually not among her favorite beverages.

"Lately I've been considering opening my own business. Maybe a restaurant."

She nodded. "It's tough to keep a restaurant going."

"Yeah. But I know the financial angles pretty well, with all the business and accounting stuff I did in school. Most businesses fail because the owners don't know how to take care of the money," he said.

"What kind of food?"

"Nouveau Cantonese Cajun," he said solemnly, but he couldn't control the smile that lurked at the corners of his lips.

"Sounds horrifying," she laughed.

"I just wanted to liven things up a bit. Work is not the most interesting of topics. Mine isn't anyway."

She shrugged. "Perhaps not interesting, but safe."

He raised his eyebrows. "Safe from what?"

"You know what I mean. Safe. Easy. The opposite of the shower conversation last night." Whoops. Now they were both going to be thinking about it again.

"Oh."

Not again. "You're always saying 'Oh.' What does it mean?"

He smiled. "It doesn't mean anything. Don't we have a reservation to get to?"

She leaned forward. "So I finally found something, however minuscule, that *you* don't want to talk about."

"See how it feels?"

She rolled her eyes. "Ha ha." Suddenly she realized that she'd not only leaned forward but had scooted closer to him. Or he'd moved. In any case, they were staring at each other, their kneecaps touching lightly. She looked down, feeling shy. When she peeked at him to see if he felt that tingling at the point where their bodies touched, he was close enough to kiss her, and he did. Slowly, pulling her toward him and tracing the curve of her waist with his palms. Her arms found their way around his neck, and she was aware of the way her breasts were separated from him only by the fabric of her jacket.

She didn't know how long they sat, his lips exploring her mouth, her neck, her hands exploring his shoulders and stomach, their beer growing warm. All she knew was that when they pulled apart gently, several of her buttons were undone, his tie had disappeared and his shirt was completely open.

They looked at each other, suspended for a moment in that post-kiss haze, where either their heads would clear and a word would break the spell, or they would fall back into a sensual trance.

His head cleared first. "That was nice."

"Yes."

"Maybe we should go, though."

"Right." She looked at her watch. "Oh no. We are so late. Chrissy's going to kill me."

They both jumped up and straightened themselves quickly. She smoothed her hair back as best she could, but the curls had already begun escaping from her smooth chignon. She removed her clasp and shook her hair out.

"I love that," Linc said from across the room, where he'd gone to retrieve his tie.

"What?" She was distracted, digging around in her purse for her lipstick.

"When you do that with your hair." He finished arranging his clothes and walked over to touch her hair gently.

She batted his hand away. "Don't start again. We'll never make it to dinner."

"Okay, okay. Maybe later, though?"

She looked at him, smiling. "Maybe."

★ ★ ★ ★ ★

When they arrived at Cam's, a tiny restaurant on the water, they could smell the spicy salmon rolls and thick sausage lasagna from the parking lot.

"I just realized I'm starving," Katrina said as they hurried to the entrance.

"It's the smell, I know. I used to work out near here, but I kept gaining weight because the smell of the red sauce drove me to order takeout all the time."

They rushed inside to find Chrissy and Rick standing by the entrance waiting for them. Chrissy frowned while Rick smiled and waved them over.

"Hey! We were about to send out the cavalry for you guys," Rick said cheerfully. He hugged Katrina and shook Linc's hand enthusiastically.

"We were about to leave," Chrissy corrected irritably.

Katrina leaned over to kiss Chrissy's reluctantly proffered cheek. "Why are you standing out here? We're hungry."

"Why don't I go get us a table?" Linc started toward the main dining room.

"Don't bother. We lost our reservation." Chrissy was not going to make this easy.

Katrina tried to placate her. "I'm so sorry. I was just running late, then Linc wasn't ready, and so I had to wait." She invented this at the spur of the moment and ignored Linc's incredulous glance at her. Rick caught it, though, and laughed lightly while Chrissy continued to glare.

"Come on, Chris, don't be mad," Linc soothed.

Chrissy softened. "Well, we've been waiting forever, so I got a little annoyed."

"We only waited for a few minutes," Rick said, winking at Katrina. "Let's just go somewhere else."

Katrina looked at Rick gratefully. "Okay. Anyone know anywhere good?"

Chrissy shrugged. "I'm not sure what's around here." She wasn't quite ready to be helpful.

"I know a great place a few miles from here. Right on the water, open late, great Thai food," Linc said. He put his arm around Chrissy. "Come on, we really are sorry. I'll even buy, and you can order whatever you want."

Chrissy laughed and shrugged off his arm in mock anger. Katrina was relieved to see that even Chrissy couldn't resist Linc's playfulness.

"One big happy family again?" Rick looked around hopefully.

"I guess," Chrissy sighed.

"Ah, so we're forgiven," Katrina said.

Chrissy turned to give her a narrow-eyed look. "This time." She grabbed Rick's hand and dragged him outside. "But I'm not buying the late excuse. Linc looks good, but not *that* good," she called out over her shoulder as she walked out to the parking lot.

Linc and Katrina looked at each other and laughed.

"It was a pretty lame excuse." Linc shrugged, holding the door for her.

She waved him off. "I didn't hear you coming up with anything. And this is all your fault anyway."

"My fault? You're the one who pranced into my apartment not even wearing a shirt."

"Wait a minute—" She stopped short as they drew close to Rick and Chrissy.

"Want to ride with us? Or do you two need some privacy?" Chrissy teased.

Rick shook his head. "Come on, let up on them, Chris," he said.

"What?" she replied, wide-eyed.

"Okay, cut the innocent act. We'll ride with you," Katrina said.

"Well, at least you'll get the backseat," Chrissy said.

"Chrissy!" Rick pulled her hand toward his Explorer.

"Oh, don't worry, Rick. I can handle her," Katrina said, sticking her tongue out at Chrissy as she climbed into the truck.

Chrissy laughed and held up a hand. "All right, all right. Let's go. I haven't had a proper meal all day."

The restaurant Linc recommended had a silly name, Try My Thai, but it more than made up for that in ambiance. The room was lit by low-hanging globes that emitted a golden glow supplemented by candles on every available surface, an eclectic assortment of tall, fat, round, square and scented wax that gave the cozy room a welcoming warmth as the temperature continued to drop outside.

The tables were covered in white linen cloths with a single silk tulip resting in a thin blue vase in the center. It was late for dinner, nearing ten o'clock, and only a few people lingered over their spring rolls and curried shrimp. They asked for a table by the window, where they could see out onto the sooty lake.

"This place is great," Chrissy said happily.

One of the things Katrina loved most about Chrissy was her ability to shift moods as the occasion dictated. Whether she was slightly annoyed or really angry, Chrissy never held on to it for long. Katrina wished she could be more like that. Instead, she tended to harbor bad feelings, hiding them away until they popped up unexpectedly at the most inopportune times.

"Thanks for thinking of it," Katrina said, smiling at Linc.

"Anyone want wine?" Rick asked, peering nearsightedly at the menu.

"How about a beer?" Linc said. "Katrina—Amstel?"

"Sure." She had a vision of herself choking down beer for years to come, all because of one first-date faux pas.

They examined the menu filled with curries, ginger stir-fry and delicate appetizers while they waited for their drinks. Katrina watched as Chrissy scooted her chair close to Rick's, asking his opinion on the difference between green and red curry, the composition of pad Thai and the similarities to Chinese food. She couldn't remember ever having eaten Thai food with Chrissy, but it wasn't too far a stretch to think this was a convenient way for Chrissy to let Rick take charge. Either way, it was working.

"She's had Thai before, right?" Linc whispered, his breath warm on her ear.

She shrugged. "You never know with Chrissy."

He smiled and rested his hand lightly on top of hers under the table. She looked at him, thinking of their earlier kiss. Their fingers interlocked.

"Ready to order?" Their waitress's hair was shaved close to her scalp, emphasizing her light bronze skin and dangling earrings. She was dressed in a loose black shift and spoke with a slight accent. They asked her for two plates of spring rolls to share and divided the rest of their order between panang curry, vegetarian pad Thai, ginger shrimp and garlic chicken with broccoli.

After the waitress glided away with their order, Katrina took a quick sip of her beer, then excused herself to the restroom. She waited a beat for Chrissy to join her, but she was too involved in debating the merits of the Merlot trend with Rick and Linc. So Katrina meandered toward the bathroom alone, glancing at the sprinkling of patrons still left in the restaurant.

As she walked to the hallway leading to the restrooms, she

noticed a plump, dark-skinned woman with a close gamine haircut sitting at a table a few feet away. The woman's face was shiny and devoid of makeup, and she wore a snug pink turtleneck with a diamond heart pendant. The woman drew her full brown lips into a polite smile as she met Katrina's gaze.

She hadn't meant to stare. She'd just gotten into one of those dazes where you can't look away, even though you don't mean to be rude. But the eye contact had gone on just a bit too long, and as she passed the woman's table, she almost felt like she should say hi or acknowledge the woman in some way. Standing in the space between the hallway and the woman's table, she glanced back one more time before grabbing the handle to the ladies' room door. For the first time she noticed the woman's companion, and Katrina suddenly felt as if she'd been caught naked on stage, lit for the world to see by an unflattering fluorescent spotlight. The woman was with Patrick.

And so she must be Jamie.

Jamie wore small oval glasses with tortoiseshell frames that gave her the air of a second-grade art teacher. Next to this round brown woman, Patrick's skin shone pale. His curly hair had grown out a bit in the weeks since she'd seen him, and it reminded her of the way it had always been mussed and unruly when they were kids. He wore a white dress shirt buttoned to the top and a dark blue jacket, and crystal Champagne flutes stood empty near their elbows. Katrina wondered what they were celebrating.

She saw the instant recognition in his pursed lips and in the glance he darted at Jamie. She tried to read the feeling in his widened eyes, but all she could clearly discern was dismay.

She wanted to stop staring, wanted to peel her gaze from his and go on into the bathroom, get out of sight, sit in the stall wishing she could climb out of a conveniently located window like they do in the movies. But it was impossible not to watch his lips curl into an uncertain smile, impossible not to feel something should be said, although she couldn't imagine what.

"Hi," Jamie said brightly, looking from Katrina to Patrick.

Patrick glanced at Jamie as if he was surprised to hear her voice.

"Hey. Um. How are you?" What do you say to the man you love and his fiancée? Patrick shifted in his seat and began tapping his fingers on the edge of his now-empty plate. "Hey. Good. I mean, I'm good. We're good." He cleared his throat. "Katrina, this is Jamie. Katrina is an old friend. We sort of grew up together," he told Jamie. At some point during this announcement, Patrick had affected a bright smile that infuriated Katrina. An old friend? Grew up together—*sort of?* She fumed.

She ignored Patrick and turned to Jamie. "It's nice to meet you," she said politely. Jamie smiled and nodded, looking curiously from Patrick to Katrina. She gestured toward a chair. "Want to join us? I haven't gotten to meet many of Pat's friends."

Pat? No one called him Pat. But this Jamie was not the perky, thin, blond cheerleader Katrina had imagined. She did not seem like the spoiled bitch Katrina had hoped for. In fact, she was annoyingly nice.

Patrick cleared his throat again, as if to warn her not to accept Jamie's invitation, and Katrina glared at him. *Pat* had a lot of nerve, wanting her to go away. He was the one who had had conveniently not told her about his engagement. He was the one who never even mentioned that this Jamie was right here in town, where Katrina might see her and get this hollow feeling in her belly.

She had wondered how it would feel to see Patrick again. She'd thought she would feel sad. She thought she would feel his absence all at once, like a chair that was snatched from under her. She had thought she would instantly miss him.

Instead, the longer she stood there and looked at him, the more she felt like slapping that stupid smile off his familiar face.

"No thanks—I'm sitting over there." She motioned toward her table and realized that Linc was looking over at her. She couldn't quite make out the expression on his face, but she smiled and waved so he would think everything was fine. She was relieved to see that Chrissy was still focused on Rick. "Well, it was good to meet you, Jamie," she said, wanting to get away. She looked at Patrick and considered saying something nasty to let Jamie know he was a cheater, a man whose friendship wasn't worth much anymore. In a way, she wanted to ruin things for him, make him feel a little of the hurt that she felt.

But she didn't. "Good-bye," she said, nodding at Jamie.

Patrick smiled weakly.

Katrina walked quickly into the bathroom, locked herself in a stall and tried to breathe slowly to make her heart stop racing. She wished she had been prepared to see Patrick, ready with some scathing comment to put him in his place. She wished she'd never seen Jamie, just kept walking to the bathroom. Maybe they would have been gone by the time she came out. Katrina hated the catty little voice in her head that told her Jamie was nowhere near as pretty as she, because this voice didn't have an explanation for why Patrick had chosen this not-as-pretty Jamie over her.

When it seemed she had been gone too long, she came out of the stall and looked at herself in the beveled mirror, making sure her face didn't show any signs of her encounter with Patrick. She smoothed down her jacket and filled her hand with water from the faucet, gulping it before heading back to the dining area.

Patrick and Jamie were not at their table when she came out of the bathroom. Linc, Chrissy and Rick sat expectantly as Katrina slid back into her seat.

"Are you okay?" Linc rubbed her ice-cold hands and looked at her.

"Sure. Why?" She tried to sound nonchalant.

"You were gone a long time."

"Yeah, I was about to come look for you," Chrissy added.

She forced a laugh. "Guys, I'm a big girl, and I just went to the bathroom." She busied herself with pouring tea into her cup and spooning in two packets of sugar.

"I guess you were talking to those friends of yours for a while, huh?" Linc said casually.

"What friends?" Chrissy asked.

"I just saw some people I knew over there," Katrina said. She drank a mouthful of tea and pretended her tongue wasn't scalded. "Mmm. This is so good," she said. "Have you tried it yet?" She directed her comment at Rick.

"Really strong," he agreed.

Chrissy helped herself to another glass of wine. Glass in midair, she paused before taking a drink. "What friends?"

Katrina felt Linc watching her. She was about to speak when Chrissy's mouth dropped open. She looked over Katrina's shoulder in surprise.

"Patrick?" Linc and Rick both turned to look.

Katrina rubbed her temples and closed her eyes briefly before turning in her chair.

"Hey," he said uncertainly. Patrick looked around the table, his nose red from the cold. "I just forgot my hat, so I came back in." He cleared his throat and shifted from foot to foot.

Chrissy looked from Patrick to Katrina.

For the second time that night, Katrina wished for a quick escape, this time a trap door underneath her seat.

Rick, oblivious to the tension, spoke first. "Hi, I'm Rick." He shook Patrick's hand energetically. "Are you a friend of Katrina and Chrissy's?"

Katrina was surprised Chrissy hadn't told him the story. She tried to meet Chrissy's eyes, but Chrissy was too busy smiling at Patrick.

"He's an old friend of Katrina's," she said brightly. "Rick's a new friend of mine."

Patrick sniffed and fidgeted. "Oh, hey, yeah, Katrina mentioned it. You must be Chrissy." He nodded and smiled, the kind of smile that tries to hide uncertainty.

"I hear congratulations are in order. The wedding's on New Year's Eve, right?" Chrissy said in a cheerful tone that made Katrina's stomach turn. She hoped Chrissy wasn't going to make a scene.

Patrick glanced at Katrina, then narrowed his eyes at Chrissy. "Yes." He said this steadily, watching Chrissy carefully.

She went on. "So, is it going to be a big wedding? Are we invited?"

Katrina felt sick. She knew Chrissy was only trying to punish Patrick a little, but thinking about his wedding made her head pound. She wanted to intervene, to stop things before they got ugly, but she didn't know how.

Patrick smiled again, but this time it was cold and did nothing to hide his anger. "This is not the time to talk about this," he said quietly.

"Well, when is a good time to talk about the fact that

you've been leading my best friend on for months, you lying—"

"Chrissy!" Katrina interrupted. She looked at Rick, who sat as if stunned by the venomous turn the conversation had taken.

Linc cleared his throat, and Patrick turned to meet his steady gaze.

Linc stood up. "Linc Davis," he said calmly, staring into Patrick's eyes. "I think you should leave."

Katrina tried to keep her mouth from dropping open. Chrissy barely stifled a laugh.

Katrina could see that Patrick was still seething over his exchange with Chrissy.

"Who the hell are *you* to tell *me* to leave?" Patrick stepped closer to Linc and pointed a warning finger at him.

Linc glanced down at the finger disdainfully. "You need to watch where you're pointing, boy."

"Boy?"

Their voices got louder, and Katrina was afraid it wouldn't be long before they were doing more than pointing and shouting. She stood and stepped between them, holding up her hands.

"Patrick, you were on your way out. So just go."

He glared at her, and she saw his eyes flick toward the low neckline of her blazer, then back to Linc, looking him up and down quickly. She unconsciously adjusted her jacket. Patrick's eyes narrowed to slits as he looked at her.

"Who's this, your new boyfriend?"

Linc made a move toward Patrick, but Katrina put a hand on his chest to hold him back.

"It's none of your business who he is," Chrissy piped in. Rick shushed her, but she waved him off.

Katrina turned toward the table. "Chrissy, shut up." She

ignored the surprised look on Chrissy's face and turned back to Patrick. "Just get out, okay? Just go."

Patrick looked at Katrina for a long beat, as if he might stay and argue, but right then the waitress walked toward their table with a heavy tray piled with food.

He shook his head at Katrina. "You sure move quickly," he spat and stalked away.

They all watched his back as he moved quickly out of the restaurant. The waitress filled their table. The food sat steaming on plates, untouched. Katrina looked down at her silverware, furious and embarrassed, trying to will her nerves to settle.

"Was he here with Jamie?" Chrissy looked at Linc, who was playing with the edges of his white cloth napkin.

"Yeah." Katrina wished she knew what to say to make Linc put down the napkin. She felt both surprised and touched that he had been ready to fight for her. It wasn't his job to protect her, but she liked that he wanted to.

"What was that all about?" Rick asked.

Was there was a way to explain, in twenty-five words or less, that Patrick was her best friend and then her lover until a few weeks ago, when the incidental information that he was already engaged came up?

"It's a long story. Maybe later?" She hoped he caught the hint.

Linc let out a long breath, but she was afraid to look at him.

Rick, ever amiable, began chatting to ease the tension. Chrissy seemed on the verge of adding something, but decided against it. Instead, she spooned rice and noodles onto her plate, passing the silver serving dishes to Rick. Once her plate was full, she tossed back her hair and looked at Katrina and Linc, Katrina unmoving, Linc still playing with his napkin. "Aren't you guys going to eat?"

"Yeah, we don't want all this great food to get cold," Rick added, then continued to chatter, trying to cover up the awkwardness with lots of cheerful words.

Katrina looked over at Linc. He set his napkin neatly in his lap and turned to her. They looked at each other, and she hoped he could see how sorry she was that any of this had ever happened. She felt his knee against hers under the table.

"Pad Thai, right?" he said softly. She nodded.

He put the noodles on a plate and handed it to her with a small smile she couldn't read.

"I'm sorry," she whispered.

He took her hand. "Let's eat."

Chapter 14

Rick slowly drove through the dark, quiet streets, making his way back to Cam's where Linc and Katrina would pick up her car. Chrissy's head rested back on the front seat as she and Rick whispered underneath the sound of Miles Davis playing on the car radio.

Katrina huddled near the window, watching the lights flick off in the lakeside mansions they rolled by. It was around 1:00 A.M., late for the families occupying these enormous houses. The roads were mostly empty—people were inside at parties and clubs, not risking frostbite in the frigid winter air. Rick had turned the heat up high, and despite the cold outside, Katrina could feel tiny pools of sweat collecting between her bra and her skin underneath her blazer and heavy coat.

She rewrote the night in her mind, over and over. In one scenario, she refused that second beer and never went to the bathroom. Another version had her and Linc arriving at Cam's on time. Her favorite featured Patrick at Mitchell International Airport with enough luggage for a trip that would take him far away from Try My Thai.

She looked over at Linc. He stared straight ahead at the back of Chrissy's head, blinking infrequently, his hands picking imaginary lint off his pant leg.

She leaned over and touched his moving fingers. "What're you thinking about?"

He stopped picking and glanced at her. "Are you mad

about me defending you?" His eyes were serious.

She shrugged. "No."

"It wasn't right for him to get into it with Chrissy, then hassle you about being out with me."

Katrina cleared her throat. "She did provoke him."

He raised his eyebrows. "You're defending him?"

She shook her head but didn't reply.

"Maybe I should ask Rick to give me a ride home," he said, looking down.

"Why?"

She wished he would look at her, make a joke, say something charming and comforting. She wished he would say that things would be okay, that he wasn't upset. She wished he would tell her that this wasn't the worst first date imaginable. She rubbed his fingers.

"If you dropped me off, you'd probably walk me to the door."

"And?"

"I'd want you to come in."

She smiled slightly. "So far, I don't see a problem."

"I just don't want to hear you say no."

"Why would I say no? Why do you think I don't want to be with you?"

He finally looked up. "Do you think Patrick will be waiting for you when you get home?"

She thought about the look on Patrick's face just before he left the table, about the way her stomach had been in knots. Katrina knew she owed Linc an honest answer and looked out the window again.

"Maybe. But he was with Jamie, so who knows?"

He sighed. "Maybe. I saw how he looked at you, how you looked at each other."

She leaned her forehead against the cool glass. She took a

deep breath, and the velvety pine smell of the car reminded her of the old red Thunderbird of her childhood. She'd felt safe in that car, seemingly impenetrable in a way she longed for now.

Linc pulled her close to him and guided her chin so she was looking into his eyes, just inches away. "You don't know how badly I want to make you forget about him. I want you to lie in my bed all night, wear my T-shirt in the morning and pretend we never saw him," he said urgently.

"Then let's. Let's go to your house." She leaned forward to kiss him but he held her away.

"But I can't pretend. And neither should you." His arms relaxed around her. She laid her head on his shoulder and felt like crying. But they were turning into the parking lot of Cam's, stopping next to Katrina's car. Chrissy and Rick got out of the car, and she put her hand on the door handle without looking at Linc.

He whispered in her ear.

"You call me next time." She nodded, feeling the tears pooling in the corners of her eyes.

Linc got out and began negotiating quietly with Rick.

Chrissy pulled Katrina aside. "I'm sorry about the Patrick thing. I just couldn't stand seeing him act like he *wasn't* a lying bastard."

Katrina wiped her eyes and tried to smile. Even when Chrissy was at her most exasperating, she tried to make her laugh. "I know." She tried to look confident and strong, but she knew it wasn't convincing.

"Want me to come home with you? We can talk about it," Chrissy said, worried.

Katrina wanted to say yes, to have Chrissy come over with her matter-of-fact advice and her eternal optimism, but she knew it wasn't the answer. "That's really sweet, but I really need to go home and get some rest."

"You're not going to act like this was no big deal, are you? You can only do that for so long, you know."

Katrina nodded. "I know."

Chrissy hugged her tightly, her dangling silver earrings cold against Katrina's cheek. "Take care. I'll call you tomorrow."

Chrissy got back into the truck where Rick and Linc waited. Katrina got into her car and drove off without looking back.

She kept the heat off during the twenty-minute drive home. She was afraid that if she felt the warm air pushing at her face she might fall asleep. And even with the CD player blasting *The Miseducation of Lauryn Hill*, her exhaustion threatened to take over.

When she pulled up to her apartment, she sat in her car awhile, her head leaning back against the seat. She turned the heat on low and sang along with Lauryn. After the song faded, she slowly made her way out of the car. Katrina couldn't wait to get inside, change into her sweatpants and the old Six Flags T-shirt she'd had since high school. She looked forward to being alone.

But she wasn't surprised to see Patrick's shadow looming large over Mrs. Collins's bare rose bushes. He leaned against the railing in front of her apartment, his skin looking jaundiced in the streetlamp's glow. This was the story of her life over the past few months, Patrick appearing on her doorstep under the heavy cover of darkness.

She stepped slowly toward him. "What do you want?" This came out whispered and hoarse. What she hadn't felt in the restaurant she felt now. The sadness of knowing things would never be the same between them.

"I wasn't sure you'd be here. Thought I might be waiting

all night." His voice was challenging.

"What's that supposed to mean?" She narrowed her eyes at him. The wind blew her hair into her face, and he was momentarily hidden from her.

"You and Linc seemed pretty cozy." He looked away into the empty street.

She couldn't believe he was standing here accusing her. A number of nasty retorts flitted through her mind, but she was too tired and cold to bother.

"Yeah, whatever, *Pat.* I'm going inside now." She opened the door and tried to step inside.

He grabbed her arm. "Wait. I'm sorry."

She wrenched out of his grasp. "You're always sorry. It's late, and I'm not in the mood, so why don't you just go back to Jamie." She moved closer to the door.

"Can't we talk for a minute?"

"What's the point?"

"Please."

Her shoulders felt heavy and tight. She just wanted to lie down, close her eyes, make Patrick and all this go away.

"Patrick, why don't you come back tomorrow, during the day? Or better yet, why don't you call first?"

He looked down at his shoes. "And say what? I'm sorry I didn't tell you about Jamie? That I don't know how things got out of control like this? That's not stuff you say over the phone or on an answering machine tape."

He met her eyes and she looked away. This was not what she wanted to hear. His uncertainty was no comfort. She shivered, her fingertips numb from the cold.

"Why should I listen to anything you say?" She leaned against the doorjamb.

He sighed and nodded. "I wouldn't blame you if you didn't. You should probably slam the door in my face. But

I'm asking you to give me a chance to talk to you. Not to make excuses, but to explain. Please."

She looked into his eyes and saw the summers they'd spent at the lake, the nights they'd spent complaining about their mothers and school and anything else they could think of.

She sighed. "Fine. But only for a while."

He followed her in and sat down quickly, as if he was afraid she might change her mind. She hung her coat on the closet door and kicked off her shoes. He still wore his jacket, but asking him for his coat might imply that she wanted him to stay.

She wanted to demand answers. How long had Jamie been in town? Did Jamie know who Katrina really was, not just some old friend? Did his mother know about Jamie? Was he still getting married on New Year's Eve? What occasion were he and Jamie marking with Champagne?

She sat back on the sofa, as far away from him as possible, watching him fidget in his seat, trying to get comfortable before giving up and sitting stiffly on the edge of the chair, his leather jacket bunched up around him.

He grabbed for a magazine, rubbed the cover, then put it down again. "I don't know where to start."

She rolled her eyes. "Why don't you just go, then? Nothing you say is going to make any difference anyway."

"But we need to talk. You don't just throw away fifteen years of friendship without talking, right?"

"I'm not the one who threw away the friendship. I'm not the one lied, who has a *Jamie* waiting for me in the wings."

He looked away. "I know. I just figured we could talk. We've always been able to talk."

She crossed her arms. "How could you do this? Why don't you start there?" She tried to stop her voice from trembling but she couldn't control the increase in volume.

He leaned back in his seat. "I didn't mean to. We were only friends, you and I. Then I came home and things changed."

The memory of the first time they made love rolled slowly through her mind. There had been none of that unfamiliar fumbling, the holding back to see what the other person would do, that uncertainty of movement and voice. She had played out the scene so many times in her head, for so many years, that it was like they had always known each other's rhythms.

"So why didn't you tell me? That first night, when I asked you where you had been, what you'd been doing?" She put her hand on her forehead and pressed, trying to block out the closeness she'd felt with him that night.

"We had already made love. How could I say it then? I mean, this is not the kind of thing you just blurt out."

She shook her head, feeling sick. "How could you have sex with me, knowing that you were lying to me the whole time?" She hated the way her voice sounded so small.

He stood up quickly and moved to the couch, sitting down close to her. Too close.

"I came just to see you, to laugh over old times, to know you again. But when I saw you standing there, looking at me, all I could think of was how much I loved you. How much I wanted you," he said urgently, trying to lock eyes with her.

She looked away.

He kept talking. "You have to know I didn't plan that. I just wanted to see you," he said. "I never meant for it to be like this."

She closed her eyes for a long moment. What did he expect her to say? Oh, it's okay, Patrick. I know you didn't mean it. Let's pretend it never happened.

"And after that? At any point during the past three months you could have told me. I asked you so many times. All you had to do was tell me the truth."

He put his head in his hands, muffling his words. "I just couldn't. The longer it went on, the harder it was to tell you. And we were having fun, weren't we? It was almost like old times."

Katrina wished she could get farther away from him, but she was afraid if she moved he might try to reach out and touch her, try to make her believe he deserved immediate and complete forgiveness.

"Does she know?" What she really wanted to know was why he'd chosen Jamie over her, why he couldn't have waited for her the way she'd waited for him in her heart. But she wouldn't ask him that. Not now.

"Jamie? No. I told her that you and I had once had a relationship but that it was long over. I don't think she suspects. She's pretty trusting."

Katrina laughed bitterly. "Poor girl."

Patrick looked angry. "You know what I mean."

"Right. You want to go along with your plans for a nice little life. You don't want me messing things up."

"Why do you have to twist my words around?"

"Why do you have to be such a jerk?"

They both sat still, looking anywhere but at each other. She stared at the thick oak bookcase she'd found at a yard sale. Dust had congealed along the shelves, creating a gray film that obscured the wood's shine. There was the book of Hemingway stories he'd brought her that first night, when he appeared on her doorstep without warning. That night seemed like a million years ago.

He spoke first. "Who's that Linc guy?"

She looked up at him, her eyes narrowed. "A friend."

"He looked like more than a friend to me."

"And if he is?"

"Then I can't see how you can be so mad at me for seeing someone else when you're obviously doing the same."

Katrina heard a roaring in her head that made her eyes water. She could almost feel her fingers curling around his neck, choking him until he swallowed those words, until he felt the way she did.

"You've got a lot of fucking nerve. For your information, I only met Linc recently. This was our first date, so as you can imagine, he and I aren't *engaged.*"

Patrick interrupted. "I shouldn't have asked you that." He held up a hand.

"What I do is none of your business." She tried to count to ten to calm down, but in her head the numbers were shouted in a staccato auctioneer's voice.

"I know. I'm sorry."

She stood up. He looked up at her and she pointed her finger inches from his chest. "You could keep saying sorry over and over for the rest of your life, and it still wouldn't be good enough. We were best friends since the sixth grade, and you ruined it because you were too weak or scared or whatever to tell the truth. So go marry Jamie, have babies, do whatever it is you want to do."

"Getting married. To Jamie. I'm not sure it's still going to happen," he said softly.

She couldn't resist. "Why not?"

He stood, and they were face to face, too close. She smelled his shampoo, the same kind he'd used since high school. She saw the coarse black hairs of his goatee. She saw the scar under his right eyebrow where she'd accidentally hit him with a Coke bottle when they were thirteen.

"Katrina. Why do you think? I really do love you."

She looked away. Maybe he meant it. Maybe it was true.

But the kind of love that wasn't honest wasn't the kind of love she wanted. She could open her arms, tell him to get rid of Jamie and forgive him. But she didn't think she'd ever be able to forget the lies he'd told with his silence.

When she looked up, his head was turned as if he was bracing himself.

"I love you, and I think you love me in your own way. But your kind of love, it isn't enough."

"I'll break things off with Jamie."

She felt her throat constrict. She thought she was doing the right thing, but she wished it didn't hurt so much.

"You could do that. But it wouldn't change anything between us. It couldn't make me trust you again."

It was a long time before he met her eyes, and when he did, his were so sad. She felt unsteady, surprised and relieved and melancholy all at once. Someday maybe it wouldn't hurt so much to look at him. Someday maybe their friendship would be a sweet memory, disconnected from this. Someday maybe she could love him without being in love with him. But not yet.

She stepped back. "Good-bye, Patrick."

He nodded slowly.

She turned and went into the bedroom so she wouldn't have to watch him leave. With all her clothes still on, she lay face down on the bed and cried.

Chapter 15

Katrina awoke at the first buzz of her alarm. Her hands fumbled around it, trying to push any button or turn any knob that would quiet the shrill beeping sound. Finally she found the right one and sighed into the silence. Nothing was worse than being jolted awake by the sound of an alarm. It was too startling, too cruel a way to start the day. And today wasn't even a workday—it was Thanksgiving. She'd just forgotten to turn off the alarm the night before.

She turned onto her back, her eyes still closed. She savored the fact that she didn't have to search her drawers for a pair of pantyhose that didn't have runs. No ironing, no rushing over the morning headlines, no waiting for the car to warm up while scraping ice off the windshield. She opened her eyes and sat up, thinking she would make herself an omelet to celebrate the fact that this was one day she wouldn't have to face her nitpicky boss.

She pulled on a sweatshirt and jeans, briefly wondering whether she could run outside to grab the paper without putting on shoes. Her mother's sometimes-I-think-you-don't-have-any-sense-at-all speech ran through her mind, and she stuffed her bare feet into her snow boots.

The whiteness surprised her when she opened the door. The walkway, the street, the world was covered in inches of fleecy snow, unmarred by even a single tire track or footprint. It wasn't too cold, just cool enough so the snow would stick, and the sky was hazy, casting shadows along the frozen streets.

She hadn't heard a thing about snow on the news the night before—John Coblan had even lamented the improbability of a snowy holiday on his eleven o'clock weather report. The drifts had sneaked up on the city, casting a damp silence over everything. Katrina knew it wouldn't be long before her neighbors dragged out their scarves and wooden-handled snow shovels to begin digging themselves out.

She was the first to break the seamless covering of snow by kicking around near her door until she felt the plastic-covered newspaper under her feet. She reached down and grabbed the paper in one hand and a pile of snow in the other. It was heavy and wet, perfect for the snowball that she shaped with her fingers. That was always the best part about winter when she was a kid—the snowball fights with her friends, her father and anyone in the neighborhood who happened to get caught in the crossfire. Blizzards provided a double bonus: the snowball battles lasted all day because schools were closed.

She tossed the snow away and went back into the house. She left her boots near the door and went to the kitchen, where she opened a fresh carton of eggs and cracked three of them into a bowl while she glanced at the headlines. She was deciding what to put in her omelet and lamenting her lack of fresh cilantro when the phone rang.

"Happy Thanksgiving," her mother sang into the phone.

Katrina smiled. Every holiday Annie was the first to call. Even the time Katrina spent Easter with Chrissy's family during college, Annie had awakened the entire Ostrowski household with her morning call.

"Hi, mom. Shouldn't you be cooking the turkey?" Katrina asked as she whisked the eggs gently.

Annie laughed. "The turkey doesn't need me watching it every second. Anyway, I'm making two turkeys."

"Two?" Katrina counted the guest list in her head. Annie,

herself, Uncle Ken, Aunt Lacey, Chrissy, Rick. Not enough for two turkeys.

Annie cleared her throat. Well, I think we're going to change things a little bit this year." Her mother's voice sounded too sweet. It reminded Katrina of the time she'd stopped in her mother's school and peeked in the door marked Nurse. She'd watched Annie pull a four-inch needle behind her back while telling the poor kid lying on the table that it was only going to "pinch a little."

"Change how? You didn't say anything about change the last time we talked." She hoped this wasn't some foolish idea, like the year Annie had suggested they eat out for Thanksgiving. Katrina had been fourteen and appalled at the idea of eating someone else's turkey.

"Don't get upset."

"Just tell me."

"Well, Charles is coming."

Katrina sighed. Sharing the holiday with Charles could be awkward, but it wasn't the end of the world. Maybe this would give her a chance to get to know him better.

"That's great, Mom." She wanted Annie to be happy. "But didn't you say he was spending the holiday with his kids in Chicago?"

"They were supposed to come to Madison, actually, to have dinner at his place."

"Didn't work out, huh?" She put salt and pepper into the eggs and set a pan on the stove to warm.

"Well, that's the other part of the news."

Oh, no, Katrina thought. She knew this had been too easy. Her mother didn't break out her sugary charm for nothing. She waited, her fingers tapping the side of the bowl.

"Charles is bringing his kids to dinner with us."

Katrina dreaded the forced small talk and fake smiles

among people who were probably just as unhappy to be meeting her.

"Don't you think it's a little soon?" she ventured.

"Katrina, Charles and I have been dating for months." No, Katrina thought. Too soon for *me*.

She knew it was selfish. She was twenty-seven. She had a job, her own apartment, credit cards. She could handle an uncomfortable night with her mother's boyfriend and his kids.

"So how many kids? How old are they?"

Annie let out her breath. "Two. Around your age, I think—I've never met them. So you're okay with it, then?"

Annie sounded uncertain. Maybe Katrina wasn't the only one who was a little nervous about Thanksgiving with Charles and his kids.

"Of course I'm fine with it, Mom. I'm sure it'll be great."

"I know how you are about change, especially around the holidays," Annie said. Her voice dripped with relief.

"Just because I refused to eat out that one year doesn't mean I'm stubborn," Katrina said.

"Right," Annie laughed. "Are you sure you don't want to invite someone, too?"

"I already invited Chrissy and Rick."

"Someone else, I meant. Like that young man I met at your apartment."

Katrina raised her eyebrows and turned off the heat under the smoking pan. She could see that she wasn't going to be eating eggs anytime soon. She'd told her mother all about the run-in with Patrick and a little more about Linc. But during the two weeks since then, they hadn't really discussed it, which was the way Katrina had wanted it.

"Oh, Mom, I don't know." She felt naked, talking about these personal things.

"Why not? You said you liked him, right?"

"He probably has plans," Katrina hedged.

"Have you talked to him?" Annie was persistent.

"Not for a few weeks." Katrina thought about the night she'd met Jamie. After a couple of days, it had hurt just a little less when she thought of Patrick. A few days more and she'd forced herself to stop imagining what Jamie had that she didn't. She'd barely flinched when she saw the engagement announcement in the paper, successfully pretending that her stomach wasn't in knots when Chrissy asked her if she'd seen it. Sometimes she thought that maybe she'd been wrong not to take him back and try to get past it all. Maybe he deserved another chance. She thought that maybe she'd expected too much, expected a storybook relationship even after they'd been apart for so long. But she was pretty sure she deserved honesty after fifteen years of friendship. She knew she was happier without those niggling doubts about Patrick, even though she still missed him. Now, she mostly told herself not to think about it when a movie or song reminded her of Patrick. She wasn't over him, but she was getting better.

But what hadn't faded was the embarrassment that made her ears burn every time she thought of Linc. She knew she hadn't done anything wrong, but their ruined date was etched in her mind. She could still see the pad Thai she'd chewed without tasting, feel the hackles on her neck when Patrick came to their table. She could smell the air freshener in Rick's truck, feel the skin on Linc's fingers as he sent her home alone.

She'd thought about calling Linc a million times, even memorized his phone number and kept track of when he was likely to be home. But she hadn't called.

"So why not call him today?" Annie said.

Katrina thought about it. There were so many reasons not

to call him. He probably hadn't spent the past few weeks sitting by the phone. And she wouldn't know what to say.

"Mom, he's probably not even home. I have to go get dressed, then shovel out my car so I can drive up to Madison."

Annie sighed. "Okay, okay. I'll see you in a couple of hours. You're going to help make the pies, right?"

Katrina got off the phone and poured her egg mixture down the garbage disposal. Her appetite had disappeared. She leaned over the sink and rubbed her hands over her face for a moment before going to dress.

Thanksgiving dinner was usually a casual affair at the Larsons', but Katrina briefly wondered if she should dress up since Charles and his kids would be there. But she decided some traditions were sacred. She searched for her favorite white fisherman's sweater and found it stuffed in the back of a drawer. Underneath the sweater was a folded-up piece of paper. She smiled when she read Linc's small, neat writing. *You owe me breakfast,* he'd written. He must have left the note the morning her mother interrupted them, that sweet, uneasy morning after they'd spent the night together. She folded the note and slipped it into the pocket of her black corduroys before pulling the sweater on over her head. She sat on the edge of the bed, brushing her hair slowly, looking at the phone. She took a deep breath and quickly picked up the receiver before she could talk herself out of it.

Her shoulders tightened with every ring. She should have rehearsed some opening line before she dialed, should have figured out what to say. But now it was too late.

The phone continued to ring and disappointment mixed with relief to leave a metallic taste in her mouth. His answering machine picked up, and she wracked her brain for a casual-yet-friendly-yet-more-than-that message.

She waited an extra beat after the tone, thought about hanging up, then worried he might guess it was her breathing on his answering-machine tape.

"Umm. Hey. It's Katrina. I just wanted to say . . . happy Thanksgiving. I guess you're out with your family or something. Okay, well, I guess that's it, then. Happy Thanksgiving. Okay, bye."

She hung up and shook her head. That had to be the lamest message ever. Had she really said happy Thanksgiving *twice?* She wished she could somehow erase it, take it back, go back to five minutes ago and decide not to call him at all. Lame message aside, she'd done it.

The snow banks were high in Madison when Katrina arrived around noon. She could hear the coarse salt crunching under her tires as she drove through the streets to her mother's red brick house. She pulled into Annie's driveway laughing—her mother already had her Christmas wreath hanging over the front door, and Katrina knew the colored lights strung through the bushes wouldn't be far behind.

Walking toward the door, she could smell the baking turkey, the peaches and brown sugar for pies, the garlic that would be folded into creamy mashed potatoes. It was colder here, and she tightened her coat around her. She noticed that icicles had formed almost artfully above the thick wooden door. She stepped inside, looking around the immaculate living room that featured a large photo of Katrina and a prom date whose last name she couldn't remember.

"Mom?" She removed her boots, making sure not to drip water on the oak floors. She turned to go shout into the bedrooms when Chrissy came bounding down the hall and nearly tackled her in a cloud of wool, blond hair and sweet perfume.

"Hey! I didn't see your car outside. Did you two sleep over

or something?" Katrina smiled, glancing at her watch. She winked at Rick, who stood just behind Chrissy wearing an apron and holding a stainless steel bowl.

Chrissy shrugged. "I figured we could help Annie taste-test all the goodies if we got here early. Where have you been?"

"It's only noon. I would have been here sooner, but my mother had me on the phone all morning." She nodded at Rick and leaned over to peek into his bowl. "What's Betty Crocker up to over there?"

Rick held the bowl away from her. "Just for that, you'll have to wait to taste this culinary masterpiece until later."

Katrina made a face at him. "Can he cook?" she asked Chrissy.

Chrissy snickered. "The only thing he's ever made me was some strange stew he claims is a Puerto Rican delicacy."

Rick cleared his throat indignantly. "Hello? I am standing here, you know."

Just then Annie swung open the kitchen door and walked briskly through the dining room with her arms outstretched. "What took you so long?" She gave Katrina a hug and a kiss on her forehead.

Katrina rolled her eyes and hugged her mother. "Whatever. I think you and Chrissy are writing your material together."

Annie waved her hand in the air. "I don't need any help with my 'material,' " she said. She tucked a piece of her long black hair behind her ear. "Now, Charles and his family will be here around four, and Lacey and Ken, too. I've got the turkeys in the oven, and we're going to get started on the pies in about an hour," she ticked off. When Annie took charge during the holidays, Katrina never put up a fight. She actually liked it when her mother ran Thanksgiving like an army drill with nothing left to surprise or chance.

Annie turned back toward the kitchen. "Rick, get back in here—we've got work to do."

Katrina watched her mother drag Rick into the kitchen and noticed that Annie was wearing a turtleneck sweater and jeans on her newly svelte frame. She was glad her mother hadn't forgotten about that part of the Thanksgiving tradition.

Chrissy and Katrina sat down on the rug in front of the TV, cracking open pecans and walnuts from the ceramic dish on the coffee table. They stared at the NFL pre-game show, mesmerized by a heartwarming rags-to-riches story about the game's top wide receiver. The sounds of Annie and Rick chatting and clinking spoons against bowls filtered out from the kitchen.

"So, talked to Linc lately?" Chrissy asked during a commercial.

"Where did that come from?" Katrina was taken off-guard. They hadn't really talked about Linc since she'd filled Chrissy in on Patrick's visit. She'd actually hoped that Chrissy had turned over a new leaf and decided to mind her own business. She should have known better.

Chrissy nodded at the television. "Bud commercial." She chewed slowly, still looking at the screen.

"Oh." Katrina wondered if Chrissy had talked to Linc, maybe seen him at Vinyl or worse, tried to intervene on her behalf. "Have you?"

"Why would I?"

"You have been known to go to his workplace, and you have also been known to butt into my life." She watched Chrissy's profile for signs that there was an evasion at work here, but she just kept chewing.

"Nope."

"No what?"

"Haven't talked to him."

Katrina sighed and realized she was actually a little disappointed. She sometimes wished she could be as fearless as Chrissy was in relationships. Chrissy would have called Linc a long time ago, and if she hadn't, well, she wouldn't still be obsessing about it.

"I called him today."

Chrissy turned to her, eyebrows raised. "And?"

"He wasn't home. I guess he's out with his family or something."

Chrissy shrugged. "I guess." She turned back to the TV and crunched open a pecan.

Katrina looked at Chrissy for a long moment. She couldn't tell if Chrissy was being suspiciously casual, or if it was just her imagination. She shrugged and turned back to the television, too. "Did my mom tell you that Charles is bringing his kids?"

Chrissy smiled. "And I bet you're thrilled about it."

"What? I don't have a problem with Charles. He seems really nice," she said defensively.

Now Chrissy laughed. "Oh yeah, it's driving you crazy, isn't it?"

Katrina relaxed and nodded. "It's just all so Brady Bunch. And I've only met him once. Next thing you know I'll be calling him Dad."

Chrissy shook her head. "Aren't you a little old to get a new dad? I mean, I know the real one's not around, but still, I don't think Annie's expecting that."

"I know. I just get all uptight when I think of my mom having this new thing going with Charles. What if he asks her to marry him? What if she says yes? What if I hate his kids?" Katrina lay back on the rug, looking up at the textured ceiling.

Chrissy leaned over her. "What if all that does happen? So what?"

Katrina didn't have an answer. She just knew it was hard to grow up and realize your mother has a life, too.

Chrissy answered for her. "You'll just get over it, get used to it, whatever. Things don't stay the same forever, you know."

A car door slammed outside. Chrissy jumped up and excused herself, mumbling about the bathroom and nuts on her face.

Katrina sat up. "What did you say?" she called after Chrissy.

"Be right back," Chrissy yelled back down the hall.

The doorbell rang. She looked at her watch. Just 1:30. Not even close to when Charles and the gang were scheduled to arrive. She clicked off the TV and walked to the door.

Linc stood with a navy blue knit cap pulled down low on his forehead and a bottle of wine clutched in his hand. He was wearing glasses with thin wire frames that made him look serious.

Her mouth hung open, and several thoughts flicked through her head at once, the most insistent being that she was going to kill Chrissy for not even warning her.

"Hey." Realizing that she'd been blocking his way into the house, she stepped aside. "Come in."

He smiled. "You're surprised to see me."

She shrugged and looked down at her feet. "I called you earlier."

He nodded. "I got the message. Happy Thanksgiving. Twice."

She laughed. "I really, really meant it."

"Do you mind if I take off my coat?"

"Oh, yeah, I mean, no, go ahead, put it right over there. And you better take off your shoes, too, or my mother might have a fit."

She sat on the couch, watching him remove his jacket,

shoes and hat. He sat down next to her, and she became aware of the silence that had enveloped the house.

"So Chrissy told you I'd be here?"

He smiled and tapped the bottle of wine against his leg. "Uh, no."

She frowned. "No?"

"Well, I got your message this morning, and I called you back, but you weren't there, so I figured you might be with your mom. So I looked up her number and called here."

"You talked to my mother?" Katrina tried to imagine what embarrassing things Annie might have said to him.

"Yeah. She told me you were on your way, and I asked her to give you a message." He set the bottle on the coffee table.

Katrina raised her eyebrows, waiting.

He shrugged. "I don't know how it happened, but the next thing I knew she was giving me directions and, well, here I am."

She didn't know whether to be furious with Annie or to go in the kitchen and give her a bear hug. She just knew she was happy to see him.

"What about your family?"

"They flew to Florida for the week."

She nodded and tried to think of how to tell him how sorry she was about not calling sooner. She saw his eyes flicker to glance behind her and she turned around.

Rick, Chrissy and Annie had congregated in the dining room behind her, smiling like a bunch of kids who'd just finished finger-painting the bathroom walls.

They sprang into action. "Linc! You finally made it. I need you to string up my Christmas lights before Charles gets here this afternoon. Rick, show him how I want them done."

"Hey, Linc, it's good to see you, man. Who're you picking in the game tonight?"

"Wine?" Chrissy teased. "I thought a bartender would bring something stronger."

Linc looked back at Katrina and smiled as Chrissy, Rick and Annie surrounded him in a whirlwind of chatter and activity. Katrina laughed and shook her head.

"Come help me in the kitchen," Annie said, putting her arm around Katrina's waist.

She followed her mother and sat down at the table to snap the string beans Annie put in front of her, carefully separating the ends into an empty plastic bag and the beans into a pot half-full of water.

Her mother picked up a pie plate and paused. "Are you mad at me?"

Katrina considered this. In the past, she might have been angry at Annie for interfering. But she shook her head. "No, I'm not."

Annie exhaled. "Good. Because I really wasn't trying to run your life. It's just that Linc called and said you had called him and I thought maybe it would be a good thing if you and he talked instead of playing phone tag."

Katrina smiled. "You could have just taken a message."

"Isn't this the message to beat all messages, though?"

They both laughed, and Annie hugged Katrina. "I just want you to be happy, honey."

"I know, Mom. By the way, how did you convince him to drive all the way up here?"

Annie turned and busied herself at the sink. "I just told him that since I'd already seen him half-naked, the least he could do was accept my dinner invitation."

"Mom!" Katrina felt her face flush with embarrassment.

Annie turned and grinned. "I only did it because I love

you. And, the more people here, the better, when I meet Charles's kids."

Katrina shook her head and laughed. "I love you, too."

After snapping the beans, Katrina put on her coat and boots and joined Rick, Chrissy and Linc outside, where the men were planning their Christmas lights strategy while Chrissy lay in the front yard making a snow angel. Katrina walked over to her. "I was so ready to kill you."

Chrissy stopped flapping her arms up and down. "I knew you would blame me," she laughed. "So, are you happy to see him?"

Katrina looked over at Linc, who was frowning and shaking his head while Rick explained something using wild hand gestures. She nodded and picked up a handful of snow. "Yeah, I'm glad he's here," she said, crunching the snow into a ball in her hands. She aimed carefully and threw it right at the back of Linc's head.

"Ouch!" He looked around, laughing. "Oh, so you want to start a fight, huh?"

Katrina waved her hand at him disdainfully. "Whatever, tough guy. I can take you." She never saw Rick doubling up with snowballs in each hand. They pelted her in the chest in quick succession.

Chrissy jumped up and yelled, "War!" and the front yard was filled with flying snow and the sounds of their shouts until Annie called them inside for hot toddies. Linc looked at Katrina and laughed at her snow-covered hair, eyebrows and lashes. She punched him playfully, and he grabbed her hand to pull her close. He kissed her on the cheek. "Happy Thanksgiving."

"Twice," she agreed. They held hands as they walked inside.

BROADVIEW PUBLIC LIBRARY DISTR
2226 S. 16TH AVENUE
BROADVIEW, IL 60155-4000
(708) 345-1325